Music Across the Wall

Music Across the Wall

Thomas J. Keevers

Five Star • Waterville, Maine

Copyright © 2003 by Thomas J. Keevers

First Edition, Second Printing

Published in 2003 in conjunction with
Tekno Books and Ed Gorman.

Set in 11 pt. Plantin by Myrna S. Raven.

Printed in the United States on permanent paper.

Library of Congress Cataloging-in-Publication Data

Keevers, Thomas J.
    Music across the wall / Thomas J. Keevers.—1st ed.
      p. cm.
    "Five Star first edition titles"—T.p. verso.
    ISBN 1-59414-074-X (hc : alk. paper)
    1. Private investigators—Illinois—Chicago—Fiction.
2. Landlord and tenants—Fiction.   3. Chicago (Ill.)—
Fiction.   I. Title.
    PS3611.E35M87 2003
    813'.54—dc22   2003049536

Dedication

To Rae, the keeper of my heart forever, and then some.

Acknowledgement

Thanks to my old CPD partner, Lieutenant Jack Lorenz, for keeping the police procedures current and the fiction honest.

Chapter One

Monday, August 7

I remember the beginning, its exact moment, the ringing of the phone. Chicago was blistering under a second week of record temperatures, and I didn't have a client to speak of. It came out of the August heat the way the first sight of land must appear to a castaway sailor. At such moments, the sailor's heart does not consider what beasts may await him on that shore. That in itself is a mercy.

I was flat on my back in the blast from the air conditioner, struggling through a set of bench presses, and by the silence following the answering machine message, I thought it was a hang-up. Then came the hesitant voice of Artemus Shumway. "Mike . . . ah, can you call me as soon as possible?" He sounded worried. Artemus never called me at home, and never sounded worried. He was the richest lawyer I knew. He paid other people to worry.

I heaved the barbell onto its cradle and snatched up the phone. "Artemus?"

"Mike, glad I caught you," he said. "Think you could drop by the office? I really need your help."

"Sure, hang on, let me grab my appointment book." I grabbed a towel instead, gave it a few seconds while I dabbed my hair and forehead. I didn't feel I was deceiving Artemus, who was a good friend. I actually did have an appointment book, but at that moment it was filled with empty, hopeful squares. "Let's see, looks like I'm free about, say, two o'clock this afternoon?"

"Mike, do you think you could come by right now? It's kind of urgent."

"Sure, I can just rearrange a couple things here, no problem." I gave it a beat. "You sound troubled, old buddy. What's going on?"

He took a couple of seconds. "We've got this death case, just sent over from another firm, it's going to trial in less than three months, and not a lick of investigation's been done. The insurance company finally yanked it from the other firm, dropped it in my lap. Expecting some kind of miracle, I guess." He sounded peeved, but miracle worker was the reputation Artemus had cultivated, over a career that spanned forty years. Miracle worker was what made him rich. That, and his magnetic charm. "Anyway, it's kind of a strange case. Guy murdered in an apartment building, over near Cabrini-Green. We represent the landlord. The claim is that the landlord let the building run into the ground, the locks on the front door were broken, a lot of crime in the hallways, drug deals in a vacant apartment, that kind of stuff."

It sounded like the landlord's liability was pretty thin; generally a landlord isn't liable for criminal attacks on his property. But there are exceptions. There could be enough here to take the case to a jury. I wasn't sure, though, what Artemus found odd.

"Artemus, that's a rough neighborhood; Cabrini-Green has the highest murder rate in the city. So what's so strange?"

"I know. That's why I need you, old friend, I need your experience." Then he added, a little self-consciously, "And your legal mind. Listen to this. The guy was a Polish immigrant. No one knows what he was doing in that neighborhood. Can't be drugs, he's just not the type. Solid family guy, typical European work ethic, worked in a machine shop all day, drove a cab at night. Busted his butt reaching for the old American brass ring, don't you know. Doesn't even own a car; no one knows how he got there. But here's the clincher: when they find his body in the hallway—his money, credit cards, everything, still in his wallet."

Now that *was* odd. "Could he have driven a fare to the building?"

"No, he wasn't driving the cab that night."

I told Artemus I'd be right over, hung up, and called to Stapler, my English setter. He cantered into the room, all grins and floppy ears. Even the most cynical judge of dogs would agree that Stapler is a beauty: perfect conformation, classic markings. If you've seen those nineteenth-century prints, the freckled Llewellyn on point, noble head, feathered tail, holding staunch as the hunter moves in to flush the bird, you've seen Stapler. That's how he looks; that's not how he acts. Stapler loves to hunt, but he does not understand my role in the enterprise. Hunting with Stapler is mainly an exercise in trying to find him, and listening to the far-off whir of flushing birds.

Out of guilt for leaving him alone so much, I gave him a scalp massage for a full minute, then let him out in the yard while I showered. As I was heading out the door I gave him a few dog biscuits and told him to stay off the couch. He gave me a freckle-faced smile that said, "Hey, no problem." He was lying.

I drove into the Loop and parked at the Hotel LaSalle Parking Garage on Washington, where I pay by the month. It's just a couple of doors from my office, but I didn't go up. I headed directly to Shumway's office, about six blocks away. Propelled, I suppose, by the prospect of gainful employment, I was walking too fast, and after two blocks my ankle was hurting like hell. An old gunshot wound. Do you hear the music? Miles Davis on trumpet, tough guy detective wends his way through the canyons of LaSalle Street, slowed only by: (beat) an old gunshot wound. Well, I'm afraid it's not how it sounds. I'm not Sam Spade, or Spencer, or even Quint McCauley. It really is an old gunshot wound, though not exactly a badge of courage. Rather it's a reminder of a sordidness which marbles my soul like fat in a cheap cut of meat. An emblem of my fall from grace with the Chicago Police Department, the end of my police career.

I slowed. If Chicago is a city of neighborhoods, the Chicago Loop is mine, and I did not want to be seen limping. I can't walk two blocks without running into at least one old lawyer friend, or maybe a copper coming from court, and I did not want to enhance the image of Mike Duncavan, Loser, to encourage the solemn eyes, the pats on the shoulder, the tinny good cheer. That was almost as bad as meeting familiar eyes which looked away. As though you were dead rather than just disbarred.

And except maybe for those occasional episodes of panic that come at dawn's early light, I'm really doing okay. It's just that I've had a few bad breaks. No; truth is, I've made some mistakes, bad mistakes. They uniformly arise with a rising of the blood. But I am getting better. Or maybe just slowing down.

I'm an ex-cop, ex-lawyer with two ex-wives. Fired, divorced, disbarred, divorced—that's the order. Still, my self-image is pretty good. S. I. Hayakawa said that man's deepest motive is not self-preservation, but preservation of his self-image—what he termed "the symbolic self." That, obviously not self-preservation, is what makes people jump on hand grenades. Though I myself am not drawn to jumping on grenades, anyone who does so in my vicinity will have my gratitude. My undying gratitude. As Popeye said, I yam what I yam.

I reached Shumway's building, three floors of which housed the mega-firm of Shumway, Goldman, and Fortuna, took the elevator to the 47th floor, where the reception area is no bigger than a dirigible hangar, ceiling three stories high, a chandelier suspended way up there like a crystal-covered Volkswagen. The receptionist did not bat a thickly painted eye when I asked for Shumway—did people usually ask for Artemus himself? She directed me to a couch, then punched in some numbers on her telephone pad and whispered into her headset.

There were about six matching furniture groups evenly spaced around the perimeter of the room, chairs and couches all in white, each with a thick oriental carpet, a glass coffee table, and a plate of English biscuits. I sat in the nearest chair. Then I looked over my shoulder, I wasn't sure why, and grabbed a biscuit. Now my attention was drawn to one feature so arresting you could not help but gawk. A tree. Not a ficus or a rubber plant, but an oak, huge, stately, branches spreading overhead like the hand of God.

I wanted to go over and touch it just to see if it was real, but an elevator door opened and out strode Artemus Shumway wearing a grin as big as New York. The last time I'd seen him, after we'd relinquished a Michigan trout stream to the fish, he was sitting on the back bumper of his brown Rolls Royce, pulling off his waders. He hadn't changed much. Tall, angular, eyes like he'd just heard a joke, he looked every bit his age, though he still had the carriage and animation of a younger man. His narrow cheeks sagged a little more than the last time I saw him, but his blue eyes were as clear as ever. He wore a starched blue shirt and a red and yellow silk tie that must have been worth the down payment on a car. I stood to shake his hand, and next thing I knew the bastard had me in a bear hug. "How're you doing, old pal?" he asked.

Releasing myself, I pointed to the tree. "Whoever said, 'Only God can make a tree' never met Artemus Shumway."

His eyes slipped sideways. "I didn't hire the decorator. Hell, I wasn't even on the committee. It's all really a bit much, don't you think?" Without waiting for an answer he was leading me in long strides down a corridor, small offices on both sides, each with an attorney nosed down at his desk. My ankle throbbed.

"I thought we might have lunch while we talked, if that's okay," he said, finally stopping at a small conference room with a "Reserved" sign on the door. He pushed it open. There was a woman standing inside with what looked like a doily on her head. Artemus nodded a greeting, then said, "What would you like, Mike?"

The woman, whose name tag read "Anita," held pencil to pad. I had no idea what the possibilities were. I wagged my head toward Artemus. "Whatever he's having."

"Tell you what, Anita," Shumway said. "Could you just bring us an assortment of stuff to make sandwiches?"

When she left, he patted my shoulder, asked how I was getting on, told me not to worry, that I had a bright future. Then he gestured for me to take a chair, pulled one out for himself, placed a brown file on the table in front of him, and sat down.

"Mike, the insurance company just sent the case over. It's supposed to go to trial soon. As I mentioned on the phone, another firm's been handling it and they've fucked it up to a fare-thee-well. There's hardly been any investigation. The discovery's done, but they did a horseshit job. Plaintiff didn't file suit until two years after the murder—on the day before the statute of limitations ran. The case has been pending for nearly three years, and now the tenants are all gone from the building. There was a fire, so the building's boarded up. I'm not even sure exactly what I want you to look for." He sat back and grinned. "But that's why I need you, old pal. Hell, I'm getting a great lawyer *and* a great investigator. How can you beat that?"

It was bullshit, but it was nice bullshit. I was wondering where the liability stood, though, and I almost caught myself giving a legal opinion, one thing Artemus didn't need. "Are you handling this case, ah, yourself?" I asked.

"Yeah." He was looking out the window.

"You going to try it? Personally, I mean?"

"Yeah." He looked over. "Why do you ask?" Then he smiled and canted his head. "Mike, I need to keep an oar in the water. It's actually been a long time since I've tried a case. They make me feel pretty useless around here."

I gathered that his partnership points had dwindled to about nothing. It's the way these big firms work, a way of keeping fresh, young blood. When you reach a certain age, your share of the power begins diminishing in annual increments. After awhile, the guy whose name appears first on the door has the least to say.

I wondered if he'd given much thought to the legal issues. "How does the liability picture look?"

"They claim the tenants complained to the landlord about broken locks on the vestibule door, but he never did anything about it. Supposedly strangers were in and out at all hours of the day and night, vagrants sleeping in the hallways. I told you about the drug deals, in the vacant apartment? At least that's what the complaint says. We've found

13

only one reported crime in the building before the murder, a robbery of a tenant. Supposedly the robber followed the tenant into the building, stuck him up outside his apartment door."

I thought a minute. The landlord's liability seemed borderline, but if he knew about prior crimes and did nothing to fix the broken locks, there might be enough to take the case to a jury. Once the jury got it, the big question was damages: how badly could the landlord get hit? I could see Artemus reading my mind.

"The deceased, guy named Tadeusz Bartodziec, left a young wife and six kids. The oldest is fifteen." Considering that each family member had a separate claim for wrongful death, which included compensation for both loss of companionship and loss of support, I guessed the potential was probably far beyond the insurance policy limits, whatever they were. I looked over at Artemus. He was reading my mind again. "The coverage is a million."

I'd pegged the client as an absentee landlord, the type who tries to squeeze as much rent out of a building as he can before it collapses in disrepair. In that neighborhood, buildings fell like victims of the Black Plague, whole blocks flattened to glass-studded dirt.

"Have you had a chance to meet with your client?"

"He was in here yesterday." Artemus grinned, seemed to relax a little, and in that instant I saw my old buddy, smiling in that way he has of finding delight where no one else bothers to look. "Moses Watson, an old colored gentleman, retired Pullman porter. Mike, wait 'til you meet him—what an interesting, delightful old guy! Talked to me for two hours, all about the golden days of railroading. I figured I could've been on one of his Pullman cars, out to Los Angeles in fifty-three. He's seventy-six. Put in forty-two years with the Santa Fe, can you believe it, Mike? Forty-two years." Refreshingly ignorant of all things politically correct, Artemus' face lit up with affection for the "old colored gentleman." Seventy-six was, I believed, Artemus' own age.

"Did he live in the building?"

He nodded. "First floor."

That was definitely a point in our favor. And he sounded like the kind of guy a jury would like. "Has anyone talked about settlement?"

"Up until two weeks ago, no. Hollis Lagatee's got the case. He never made a demand, you know how he is. So the insurance company never made an offer."

I knew how Hollis was, and how insurance companies were. The companies never make the first move in settlement negotiations. They have the power to sit back and wait for the plaintiff's lawyer to make a demand, confident he'll eventually blink. But lawyers like Hollis Lagatee don't blink. "So where does it stand?" I asked.

"I called Hollis the day I got the file, pushed him for a demand. Since the company wouldn't make an offer, I was surprised he made one, but he did. He wants three million."

"Three million? I thought you said the insurance policy was one million."

"I know. Three million's his demand."

"What the hell does he want, the old guy's pension?"

Artemus shook his head. "I think they want the building, old friend. Only thing Moses Watson's got in the whole world."

"What does anyone want with a boarded-up building in that neighborhood?" It stood in the shadow of Cabrini-Green, one of the most crime-infested public housing projects in the country. Not the kind of neighborhood you go cruising to find a friendly bar.

"There's been a lot of talk about tearing down the projects, Mike. Think about what a prime location that would be, a mile from the Loop. In neighborhoods right next door to Watson's, they're already re-habbing all over the place. Have you been in that neighborhood lately?"

I shook my head. "Not since I left the police department."

"It's turning into yuppie heaven, for God's sake. Right now, his building would go for about a million, maybe more. Boarded up or not."

I went to the window, looked out over ranks of lower buildings like up-ended shoeboxes marching toward Lake Michigan. In the distance, white sails scattered on the blue water like butterflies. I wondered again why Artemus was handling this case personally. Not that it was a small case, but this was Artemus Shumway, legendary trial lawyer, the guy magazine editors loved to do feature articles on. Did Artemus see this one as his swan song?

There was a knock at the door, and without waiting for an answer Anita pushed in a cart piled with sliced roast beef, cold cuts, cheese, and cookies as big as saucers.

We made sandwiches. I poured a can of Coke into a cut crystal glass, tonged ice cubes out of a silver ice bucket. When we sat down I said, "How much time do we have?"

"Not much. The case was scheduled to go to trial next week. I had to practically get on my knees to the assignment judge to get a continuance. She gave us three months. Trial is set for October twenty-second. The other side won't waive the sixty-day rule, though, so we've only got fifteen days to complete the investigation."

"Fifteen *days?*" Intended to prevent unfair surprise, the sixty-day rule holds that neither side can come up with new

16

evidence within sixty days before trial. No matter how good the evidence may be, if it wasn't disclosed before the cutoff date, it cannot be used. While the parties often waive the rule, they do so when it is to their mutual advantage. Bad as Hollis Lagatee's own case might be at this point, he must have thought he had Artemus over a barrel.

Artemus pumped his head. "I know. Counting today. Last day is August twenty-second." He squinted over at me. "You get along pretty well with Lagatee, don't you?"

Coming out of law school about the same time I did, Hollis Lagatee rose like a comet among successful personal injury lawyers, and now he counted among the Big Five in high verdicts. An honorable guy, his closing arguments would put you in mind of a parish priest chatting with his parishioners: down to earth, just a hint of sanctimony, with a big overlay of common sense. Juries loved him.

"We worked together on a bar association committee," I told him. "I helped him put on a seminar, the year he was chairman. What's he got in the way of witnesses?" I ate the last bite of my sandwich, walked over to the cart, took a chocolate chip cookie.

"He's listed only one witness, supposedly a former tenant, but Watson says he's never heard of her." He pulled a document from the file, looked it over. "Her name's Shavonne Sykes. They say she complained to the landlord about the broken locks, and strangers in the building, and the dope dealing—the whole business. But when our predecessor firm subpoenaed her for her deposition, she'd moved, and they couldn't find her."

"Wait a minute," I said, cookie halfway to my mouth. I put it down. "Then Lagatee's office can't find her either?" Lagatee had to cooperate in finding the witness; otherwise he could be barred from calling her to testify in his own case. "Seems like Lagatee's playing some high stakes poker, not waiving the sixty-day rule. If she doesn't turn up within sixty days before trial, they can't use her."

Artemus shook his head. "Actually, the court's already ruled in their favor on that point. When no one could find the witness, our predecessor firm moved for summary judgment, since Lagatee basically had no witnesses. The motion was denied."

A motion for summary judgment is just what it sounds like—if the defendant believes that the plaintiff doesn't have the evidence necessary to prove his case, he can ask the court to summarily dismiss it without going through a full trial. In the beginning of a lawsuit, in the "discovery" stage, both sides have to turn over all of their cards. If the defense lawyer can point to the plaintiff's hand and say, *Look, Judge, that's all he's got, there's not enough there to prove a case*—if you convince the judge of that, plaintiff's outta there. Time to fold 'em, ball game's over, fat lady sang, case dismissed.

But good judges are reluctant to grant summary judgment unless it's absolutely crystal clear that there's not enough evidence to support a case. A great deal depends on the judge you draw. There are some who will arrogantly relegate to themselves decisions that should be left to the jury; there are others, afraid to make a decision, who consistently pass the buck, denying the motion even when the right to summary judgment is clear as gin. And there are a few, like Judge Bronstein, who reads the briefs and does his homework and you know when you stand before him that bullshit will get you nowhere. His questions are pointed, and you better have the right answers or you lose, no matter what side you're on. He calls them as he sees them and when he rules he tells you why, unlike judges who, either because of arrogance or cluelessness or fear of reversal, simply declare, "I have ruled."

"Did the judge give a basis for denying the motion?"

"Yeah. The basis was a statement of an investigator who'd interviewed the supposed witness."

"But that's hearsay."

"I know. But the judge said he wouldn't apply the rules of evidence that technically since it wasn't a trial, and it wouldn't be fair to the plaintiffs to enter summary judgment against them just because they'd temporarily lost track of a witness. He said that as far as he was concerned, if she doesn't show up at trial, we still have a remedy; we can move for a directed verdict then. So our predecessor firm tried a slightly different tack. They brought a motion to bar the witness from testifying at trial since they'd never had a chance to take her deposition. The judge denied that, as well. Said she wasn't under plaintiff's control, and the motion was premature."

I shifted gears. "You said no one knew why Bartodziec was in the building. Don't they have to prove that the guy was lawfully on the premises?" I was working off the top of my head, but if Bartodziec was a trespasser, the landlord would have no duty to protect him from anything, other than maybe to refrain from shooting the guy himself. The plaintiff has the burden of proving every element of his case, which would seem to include proving that Bartodziec was legally there.

Artemus laughed. "Just like I said, Mike, still a top-notch lawyer. I've already filed another motion for summary judgment on exactly that issue. Plaintiffs can't meet their burden of proof if they can't prove what Bartodziec was doing there. It's all briefed, hearing's set for next week."

I chewed a bite of chocolate chip cookie. There was probably no specific case precedent which held that the plaintiff had to prove the deceased wasn't a trespasser. Still, it made sense. The duty the landlord owed to the deceased depended on whether or not he was lawfully on the premises. But that argument was thin and technical, and somewhere back in the disorganized closet of my brain, some precedent was trying to get my attention. While it wasn't connecting, I had a feeling it was against us. I asked Artemus: "Have you found any case law? On the trespasser issue, I mean."

His smile faded. "No, just general burden of proof cases. But Lagatee's got a tough burden. He's also got to prove that the broken locks were a cause of the murder."

I agreed that Lagatee had a pretty thin case—surely he knew that. But I knew Lagatee. He was just hoping to make it to the jury. If Hollis could stand before those twelve citizens good and true, tell them how the slum landlord's greed robbed the little children of a father, he knew he had a chance of hitting one more out of the ballpark. But could he get to the jury? He had to put on proof first. It was meager.

Artemus' motion was meager, too, but I supposed he had nothing to lose. I didn't say anything to him, but I didn't think a judge was likely to let an abstract legal principle like that one—that plaintiff can't prove Bartodziec was not a trespasser—deprive the widow and fatherless children of their day in court. At least, since the case was on the trial call, his motion would be heard by a different judge than the one who'd heard the prior motions brought by the former firm. Then that flash of memory came again, a case on point back there somewhere. A trespasser in a railroad station?

Artemus laced his fingers behind his head and leaned

back, studying one corner of the ceiling. By the look on his face, he knew as well as I did that the chances of winning the motion for summary judgment were dismal. Then he turned, looked straight at me. "Maybe you could work with me on this on the legal side, since you've got a pretty good relationship with Lagatee."

I shifted. "Artemus—I can't practice law, you know it." I felt trapped. Actually I could assist him, as a sort of glorified paralegal. It wasn't pride that kept me from saying yes. I'd made a commitment to myself not to work for less than a hundred dollars an hour. I was selling my legal expertise, not as a lawyer, but as an investigator who'd been a trial lawyer, trying to develop an image as well as a reputation. At the moment I may have been a little down at the heels, but there was no one in town who could match that combination. I'd been kicked off the cops, sure, but no one ever said I was anything less than a first-rate detective. And my disbarment had nothing to do with my lawyering skills. I just get a little impulsive at times. My fuse fell into the "short" category, a trait which has not helped me advance toward my life goals.

In certain kinds of lawsuits—big, expensive ones—an investigator who knows both the street angles and the legal angles can save a client a lot of money. Not that I give legal advice—I could go to jail for giving legal advice. But in my last two cases, trial work was not the lawyers' specialty. They had a good grasp of the legal issues, but they were looking at the wrong picture. That is, until I started developing their cases.

So what to tell Artemus? Even though clients weren't knocking down my door, I had my image to consider. But then came the deciding factor: this was my old friend, a guy who stood by me when others pretended not to know me.

"Okay," I said. "I won't charge you full boat unless I'm investigating. When I'm doing paralegal work you get me at the paralegal rate."

His mouth opened slightly and his eyes softened—that sympathetic look again. I shook my head. "Artemus, it's not a problem."

He snatched up his wrist as if he'd touched a hot stove and looked at his watch. "Damn, I'm late for a board meeting. Listen, sorry to run off like this, but wait here, my secretary will bring you a copy of the file."

As I waited, I couldn't help but notice how much food was left on that cart. I took two chocolate chip cookies, slipped one into each coat pocket.

Chapter Two

Back on the sidewalk, the heat hit my face like warm cotton candy, and for some reason, as sweat oozed around the band of my straw hat, the name of that case came to me: *Rhodes v. Illinois Central Railroad.*

In the dark, early hours of a frigid January morning, a rail commuter found a man surrounded by empty beer cans asleep on the floor of the station house. When the commuter boarded the train, he reported the sleeping man to the conductor, who reported it to the railroad police, but later in the morning, when the conductor made the reverse trip, the man was still lying on the floor, and he reported it again. Because of a series of miscommunications, the man laid there until noon, when the Chicago police finally came and took him to a hospital.

The man's name was Carl Rhodes, a college student who'd last been seen partying with friends the night before. He'd suffered a massive head injury, though no one ever knew the cause, for shortly after arriving at the emergency room, Carl Rhodes died.

Carl's mother sued the railroad for negligence. As best I could remember, the case went to the Illinois Supreme Court. I couldn't remember how it ended, but I seemed to recall an issue of whether Carl was a trespasser.

I made a detour, stopped at the law library, looked up the case citation, located the numbered volume from the shelf, and perused the case in a comfortable chair near the window. My memory was correct. There was a trespasser issue. The lawyer for the railroad argued that plaintiff had

the burden of proving that Carl was there for a lawful pur-
pose, and since no one knew why he was there, the railroad
was entitled to summary judgment. The Illinois Supreme
Court disagreed:

*With respect to whether plaintiffs established that Carl
Rhodes was not a trespasser, we find that the evidence raised a
jury question on the issue of Carl's status on Illinois Central's
premises. Where the facts surrounding the issue of a plaintiff's
status on land are disputed, or different inferences may be drawn
from the undisputed facts, the plaintiff's status is a question of
fact to be resolved by the jury.*

So there it was. If Carl had been a trespasser, the railroad would have no duty to rescue him, but it was up to the
jury, not the court, to decide whether he was or he wasn't.
Artemus probably didn't know about the *Rhodes* case, at
least not the trespasser issue, and it didn't take me long to
decide not to tell him. Probably Hollis Lagatee didn't know
it either, or he would have cited it in his brief and Artemus
would have mentioned it. The case would give Lagatee just
what he wanted, a chance to stand before those twelve ju-
rors and persuade them to give his client a great deal of
money.

A lawyer has an ethical obligation to inform the court of
any precedent he finds which is adverse to his own position.
Precedent such as this one. But not *lawyers* such as this one
because—ta-da!—I was not a lawyer. I was not one of those
permitted to inform the court of anything. Rather, I was
one who could go to jail just for trying. Besides, this case
was distinguishable, somehow. The railroad's alleged negligence was not in failing to protect Rhodes from attack, but
in failing to help him once he was discovered in his helpless
condition. That wasn't the case with Bartodziec.

I walked back to my office, the thin file under my arm

reminding me of how unprepared the case was, thinking that even if the trespasser question was up to the jury, Lagatee had to persuade the jury that Moses Watson's negligence was a cause of Bartodziec's death. But there was no greater maestro at playing upon a jury's heartstrings than Hollis Lagatee. Unless it was Artemus Shumway. They were two giants, both with weak cases, both playing for high stakes. If Lagatee didn't find his only witness before trial, it was all over for him. But if he found her, the odds would roll over in his favor like a beer barrel in a rowboat; Lagatee would have all twelve sniffling in their hankies.

The five-story stone structure that houses my office squats among the high rises at the fringe of the Loop, a fugitive from the wrecking ball. Some people would call it dingy, people with no sense of aesthetics. As an architectural critic might say, the iron framework of the fire escape sings a duet with the steel girders of the elevated structure. Actually the el sings much louder, but you get used to it. The style is neo-classical, Greek columns flanking the windows, the buckskin-colored facade covered with all kinds of ornamental friezes.

I went in on the Wells Street side, as usual taking the stairs instead of the elevator, which is about the size of a fat man's coffin, and the lurching makes you think you're being carried to your final resting place. My office door is mostly textured glass with a mail slot at the bottom and the name of my company in big black lettering: Legal Investigations, Inc. I know: as my first wife Beth would say, "Truly imaginative, Mike." Well, I never claimed to be creative. Beth was the creative one—and now she was growing wealthy at it.

Inside I picked up the mail off the floor and dropped it on the receptionist's desk. I don't have a receptionist, but if

I did, she'd use this desk, in the waiting area where people would wait if I had people waiting. The former tenants left behind the furniture they didn't want. Sixties functional, I guess you'd call the style. I made a mental note that I really, really needed to dust.

As President, CEO, and employee of the month, I rate the single private office. Aside from a picture of Beth on the credenza, the office is without ornament. I tossed the Bartodziec file on my desk, put on a pot of coffee, and checked the answering machine for messages: zero.

When the coffee was done I poured a mug, sat in my chair, and turned to the window, the best feature of my office. The corner of the building is sliced away to form a slim fifth side where my window is, facing diagonally across the intersection under the elevated tracks toward the fast photo place on the opposite corner. When the train passes, the wheels rumble along not far above my head, but it's gotten so I don't even notice. There's a good view north down Wells Street, and to the east I can see all the way to City Hall.

On a scale of views, it's at the opposite end from Artemus' lofty one, with the city and Lake Michigan spread at his feet. I like mine better, up close and personal, a human fishbowl, cars and buses and taxis, people on the sidewalk streaming past, piling up just below my window to wait for the light. I'm only about fifteen feet above the crowd, but no one ever looks up. I sit here and study their faces unnoticed. In the summer, hordes of secretaries in their low-cut outfits bounce past directly below, unconscious of the lascivious beast lurking above. Yes, I'm a dirty old man. Yes, I'm a sexist pig. But I love myself even so.

I turned my chair around and opened the file on my desk. It looked like Watson's prior attorneys did little more than go through the motions, which may not have been their fault. They can only do what the insurance company will pay for. There were routine answers to interrogatories filed by both parties. There were two transcripts of deposition testimony, one of Moses Watson, one of the widow.

I pulled out Mrs. Bartodziec's deposition first. The widow described in some detail what a hard-working man Bartodziec was, how good a husband, how terribly she missed him. How the children could not get over their father's death. He had been a devoted father of six. At the time of her deposition, nearly three years after his death, the vacant place at the head of the dinner table still spread gloom among the family. During the widow's deposition, Moses Watson's former lawyer frequently asked her if she wanted to take a break—a sign that she was breaking into tears regularly. No doubt about it, a jury could run away with this one. Tadeusz had worked in a machine shop, drove a cab part-time. They lived frugally, saved every nickel, hoping to start their own business one day. Tadeusz was the one who handled the money, and he was rather secretive about it. After he died, though, it turned out he'd just been salting it away in a plain old savings account at minimal interest.

She said she had no idea why Tadeusz was in Watson's building on the night of the murder. He'd come home from work as usual that evening. They had dinner, then Tadeusz said he was going out for a little while. He was not driving the cab. He did not say where he was going, and she didn't ask. She said that was not unusual. It was the last time Tadeusz Bartodziec's family saw him alive.

Moses Watson's deposition was much thinner. He seemed defensive in his answers, kept insisting he'd kept a nice building, even when he wasn't asked. I couldn't blame him, but it only made him sound more guilty. He said he didn't know of any crimes in the building prior to Bartodziec's murder. He denied that tenants had asked him to fix the lock on the front door, or that he knew it was broken.

One of Lagatee's associates had taken the deposition, a name I didn't recognize. For some reason he never asked Watson about drug deals out of the vacant apartment. Probably just an oversight. He spent a lot of time asking questions about the building, though: did he own it outright, what was its condition, had it recently been appraised, were there any mortgages, any liens, had he received any notices of building violations. There was no doubt about it; they were going after Watson's building.

There was a report from the plaintiff's economist, about twelve pages of graphs and statistics. Bottom line: the purely economic loss of the father's earning capacity to the family was less than a million dollars. That of course accounts for only *economic* loss, the (supposedly) strict dollars-and-cents required to compensate the family for the loss of the father's income. In a case like this, it was the smaller component of damages. The big ticket items were in the claims of the widow and each of the fatherless children for the loss of the father's society. In that sense, it was a personal injury lawyer's wet dream. I figured the world's most conservative jury wouldn't award less than $500,000 each, plus, say, another million tacked on for economic loss. That came to 4.5 million. And that was a *conservative* jury. Goodbye building.

Loss of society is brought home to the jury through heartbreaking little reminders of what the loss of one human being can mean to another. The evidence was there in the file, turned over in discovery. There were copies of letters written by Tadeusz to his wife, birthday greetings to the kids, graduation cards, all written in Polish, with a translation stapled to the back. There were lots of photographs: a grinning family in front of a Christmas tree; Tadeusz horsing with the kids on the living room floor; Tadeusz taking a small fish off the hook for one of the kids.

There was one of Tadeusz and his wife looking into each other's eyes, wrists draped around each other's necks. She was pretty: slender with shoulder-length blonde hair, and dimples which gave her a mischievous look. He was built like a beer barrel, short and stocky and balding, with massive arms and a bashful smile.

As I sorted through the photocopies of the birthday cards, I noticed on some of them the carefully sculpted, rhinestone-studded nails of the secretary who had stood at the copy machine. I could almost picture her wearily placing one after another on the glass, indifferent to these milestones of human caring. Most of the cards were not signed as you might expect of a father with so many kids— no simple "Love, Dad." On all of them, Tadeusz had taken the time to write a little note in Polish.

I got up, stretched, poured another cup of coffee, then started reading the police reports. The beat car had responded to a call of shots fired in the second floor hallway at about ten-fifteen p.m. They found Bartodziec alive but unconscious, lying in a pool of blood. He was removed by ambulance to the emergency room with a gunshot wound to the chest, and was pronounced dead on arrival. The reporting detectives went directly to the scene, protected it until the crime lab got there. They found one spent cartridge casing on the stairs below where the body had been lying. One bullet was recovered from Bartodziec's body.

The detectives interviewed Fannie Walker, the woman

on the third floor who had called the police. She said she'd been watching television when she heard loud voices in the hallway. She didn't pay any attention at first, but when they got angrier, she went to the door and listened. She could not hear what they were saying. She did not open the door. It sounded like there was a struggle, then she heard a shot, and she called the police. They were definitely men's voices, but not voices she recognized. The detectives knocked on doors, listed the tenants they interviewed. No one was able to tell them anything more. They found no eyewitnesses.

There was a supplementary report, showing they interviewed neighbors in the surrounding buildings the following day. None of them knew anything, either. There were no crime lab reports or photos in the file, so I called Shumway's office, reached his secretary, and asked her to tell Artemus to subpoena the records from the police crime lab.

It was late afternoon when I put all the papers back in their manila folders, stuffed them back in the file. I dialed Moses Watson's number, reaching him at home on the first try. He said I could come right over. I headed for the parking garage, just past The Loan Arranger Pawn shop, tastefully tempting passersby with a window full of neon. Three gold pawnbroker balls wink in sequence, $Instant Cash$ flashes in green and !We Buy Gold! in red, and glowing blue diamonds bracket the words "Custom Jeweler." A hand-lettered sign pasted in the lower left corner says that The Loan Arranger will even sell you a pager.

As a faithful monthly customer, the LaSalle Hotel Parking Garage grants me a space on the first floor near the exit, with in-and-out privileges. The establishment is not an adjunct to the LaSalle Hotel, but happens to be the gutted remains of the old hotel itself, a five-story, hunkering structure of dark masonry that seems to draw down weight from the sky, now providing lodging for motor vehicles instead of people. If you stand across the street and look up at one of the open windows, you might expect to see the ghost of some long-ago traveler staring down at the passing traffic; what you will actually see, framed by the peeling paint of the open window, is the back end of a Ford or a Chevy. The lobby still has the look of a third-rate hotel, though: a front desk with bored clerk, cheap knotty pine paneling, and a line of dimple-walled phone booths.

Chapter Three

I turned my '84 Dodge Omni west on Randolph, then north on Halsted. It's a maroon hatchback, a little rusty along the rocker panels, and the passenger side window doesn't roll down, but it's still ticking along after 182,000 miles. Some so-called friends are given to making wisecracks about my car, completely ignorant of the fact that it was *Motor Trend Magazine*'s 1984 Car of the Year. It had been my first wife's car; she got my Lexus. For some reason I kept the car even though, giddy in mid-life crisis, I bought a brand new, cherry-red Corvette as soon as the divorce was final. It was a good thing I kept the Omni. In the detective business, you don't want to be drawing attention to yourself nosing around city neighborhoods in a conspicuous car like a Corvette. And anyway, my second wife took the 'Vette.

I met her, a drop-dead gorgeous, part-time model, at the dealership where I bought the car. She was the cashier in the service department. She told me she admired my taste in cars, and we just hit it off. Now she's got the 'Vette, though I still have the payments.

Watson was renting a new townhouse on North Larabee, and after I parked I stood on the sidewalk for a minute, marveling at the change in this neighborhood, just a few blocks from the building where Bartodziec was murdered. Not long ago, it was a wasteland—abandoned buildings, abandoned refrigerators, abandoned cars, abandoned lives. You could buy dope on any corner, if you could work up the courage to come down here. It had been a violent no-man's-land you wouldn't even want to drive through.

Now a neat row of townhouses lined the sidewalk, brand new, red brick, each with a small, emerald patch of lawn and a wrought iron fence. I found Watson's, went through the unlocked gate and rang the bell. The methodical undoing of locks seemed to take a full minute, then the door swung open, and Moses Watson stood in the doorway, ebony-skinned, close-cropped, ivory hair, carefully trimmed mustache, rimless spectacles, white shirt without a tie. He introduced himself, smiling wearily, ushered me into the living room, directed me to a chair. "Can I get you some lemonade?" he asked.

"If you're having some."

"I just made it." As he disappeared toward the back of the house, I looked at my watch. It wasn't too early for a cocktail, but he hadn't offered. The room was as clean as a funeral parlor, smelled of furniture polish. An old clock ticked. There wasn't much furniture: a couple of easy chairs, a couch, a round table with a lamp at the window. In the foyer, though, two entire walls were covered with photographs and old posters.

I went over for a closer look and, scanning those framed memories, I came to understand how Artemus was so taken with Moses. There were pictures of uniformed Pullman porters, streamlined locomotives, railroad stations of long ago. There was one photograph of Eleanor Roosevelt boarding a train, a young, brass-buttoned porter standing at the foot of the stairs, extending a hand. Both had bright smiles: his was dignified, hers a little silly. He had a trimmed mustache and square jaw, like Watson's.

Watson came back into the room, saw what I was looking at, and grinned.

"That's you, isn't it?" I pointed to the Eleanor Roosevelt picture.

He nodded, handing me a lemonade. "A very fine lady she was," he said, looking over his glasses. "Fine lady." Then his hand fluttered to another photograph, Watson in uniform, standing next to a middle-aged black man in a business suit. "Know who that is?"

I shook my head. "Don't think so."

"A. Philip Randolph, he founded the Brotherhood of Sleeping Car Porters!" He pointed to another one, a group of porters gathered around a man in a business suit, probably a much older Randolph. "That was the twenty-fifth anniversary of the brotherhood. New York, nineteen-fifty. That's me, standing next to Mr. Randolph." Watson was holding an American flag, and everyone looked solemn.

He turned to the other wall. "That there's the Super Chief," he said, pointing to a faded poster, a streamliner rounding a bend somewhere in the American West. "She was my baby for forty years. You know, I can count on one hand the number of times she was late?" He spread his fingers. "Less than five, in all those years. Those were good years," he said sadly, then his eyes began to drift, went to the carpet. He seemed to have forgotten what he was saying. He looked at me. "Good years," he repeated. I did not understand how a black man who rode those trains through the darkest days of Jim Crow, bowing to the white man, scraping for tips, could call those "good years;" yet if you looked at the dignified faces in those photographs, you could see that their pride was palpable. It occurred to me that to say work dignifies a man is only half the equation; man also dignifies work.

"Can we sit down and talk?" I said.

He chuckled, nodded his head. "Of course, of course. Mr. Shumway's secretary called me, said you'd be in touch." He took a piece of paper from his shirt pocket, looked at it. "Mister . . . how do you say your name?"

"Duncavan. Mike Duncavan."

"Duncavan. Well, please sit down. You didn't come here to listen to a sentimental old fool talk about the railroad." He took my elbow, directed me to a chair as if he were assisting me to a train seat, and sat on the couch.

"Mr. Watson, can you tell me where you were the night the man was shot?"

"Please, call me Moses. I was in Atlanta, visiting my sister. I was down there about two weeks."

"Can you give me a list of the tenants?" They were on the police report, but I wanted to see his own list.

"I got to think about it. I didn't have any leases. See, of all the buildings on the block, mine was the best, it really was. Maybe the best in the whole neighborhood. I didn't have a lot of turnover." His thoughts drifted off somewhere. I waited. "Let me tell you something, Mr. Shumway—"

"Duncavan." I would have let it go, but I wanted to be sure he was with me.

"Duncavan, sorry. Let me tell you something. My wife and I bought that building in nineteen forty-seven. It was our dream. Oh, it was a fine place, and we kept it nice. Or we tried to. I was travelin' all the time, but Cassie, she worked hard, keeping it clean and nice. Vacuumed the hallway carpets 'least once a week. Back then, all my tenants had jobs. Then things changed, the neighborhood turned bad, filled up with sorry ass, no-account niggers." He looked at me. "Sorry."

I shrugged.

"But you understand? It wasn't just our block, the whole neighborhood. Gang-bangers up and down the streets, killin' up people. Tearin' up your building just for devilment. People 'fraid to go out the house. And mail boxes?

You couldn't keep mail boxes, they'd rip them right out the walls. Get new ones, fix 'em, you find 'em tore up the next day."

He gave me five names of former tenants, ticking them off slowly, struggling to remember. I jotted them down. There were six apartments, two on each floor. He lived in 1 South. That accounted for all of them.

"What about vacant apartments?"

"I never had no vacant apartments."

I looked at his eyes: rock steady. "You're sure? They're saying that one of your apartments was vacant. People dealing drugs out of there."

"I know, but that's just crazy. I never had no vacant apartments."

"What about when a tenant moved out? You must have had to find a new one?"

"No, no. I tole you, people was just waiting to move in, that's how nice a place it was. That's why I didn't have no leases. Didn't need any. Soon as someone moved out, someone moved in. We didn't have that many people move, anyhow."

"What about the lock on the front door? Was it broken?"

"I don't think so. Sometimes things break. When they do, I try to fix 'em. I don't remember it being broke, though."

"Do you remember anyone ever complaining about the lock on the front door not working?"

"I can't recollect, but if they did, I would of fixed it."

"Do you know where any of the tenants are now?"

He shook his head. "Scattered with the wind. I haven't seen any of them in two, three years. If they was able, they got out of this neighborhood. They wasn't no other buildings like mine."

"Mr. Watson, it's important that we find them. I'm going to ask you to do whatever you can to help. Why's the building boarded up?"

"Had a fire, two years ago. I'm tryin' to get it fixed up, but the insurance company's giving me a bad time. They say there's not enough insurance, and we're fighting about that. I can't start the work until I get some money."

"I should get a look at the building. The sooner the better."

"Sure. You want me to come along?"

"It's not necessary. If you could just get me a key?"

He left the room, returned in a couple of minutes, handed me the keys. "You got a flashlight? There's no electricity."

"Yeah, I do."

He sat down heavily, as if a great weight bowed his shoulders. His eyes flitted across the carpet in search of something. "Mr. Duncavan, I—"

"Please, it's Mike."

"Mike." He looked at me steadily. "I'm ole, Mike. It costs money. After Cassie passed, I had trouble keeping the place up. You know what? I'm just pleased she doesn't have to go through all this worry. It'd break her heart." His gaze drifted across the room. "Thing is, I got a daughter, down in Georgia, and grandkids. My son-in-law's a minister, an educated man. A *good* man. Coulda stayed up here and done right nicely, but he was called to do the Lord's work among the poor folk down there. Got hisself a little church, but they don't got much else." A vapor of a smile touched his lips. "They poor as church mice, you could say. Anyway, guess you know what I'm getting at. Sure'd be nice if I could leave them something. The building ain't much now, all boarded up, but I hear it could be worth some real money if I just got it fixed up."

He paused again. I waited. "You know, I did have some building violations, nothing too serious."

"Did you get them fixed?"

"Some I did, but then we had the fire, and now the City's been threatening to tear it down. I got a lawyer, working on that. McGarry's his name." A smile flickered over his face. "You know Mr. McGarry? I can't recollect his first name." His eyes shifted, trying to remember. "He got a downtown office."

"Daniel McGarry?"

"Yeah, that's him. He takin' care of things in court. He says it all takes time. Lucky thing, he got me the good insurance. You know him?"

The chances of my knowing a lawyer who practiced in housing court were pretty slim, but I knew Danny McGarry. In my mind's eye, I pictured Danny wearing a big, gold ND sweater. A boyish "double domer"—Notre Dame undergrad and Notre Dame law—he still had that collegiate way about him, and every weekend in season, he still drove to South Bend for the home games. Danny had an office over in whiplash towers across from the courthouse, worked a general practice, a few personal injury cases, nothing big, and was given to pro bono work for a variety of causes. A couple of times, we'd been adversaries, cases that settled before trial.

"Is it okay with you if I talk to your lawyer?" I asked. "Mr. McGarry, I mean."

"Sure. You're my lawyer too, ain't you?"

I caught myself starting to say yes. "No, Mr. Shumway's your lawyer. I'm an investigator, Mr. Watson. I work for Mr. Shumway."

He smiled. "Please, it's Moses. All the same, it's good to

have two lawyers helpin' me." Not wanting to offend, he added, "*And* a good investigator."

Something he told me had spurred another question. I tried to recall what it was. I thought it was something about insurance, but that didn't quite satisfy. Still, I wanted to have a look at his insurance policies, see if there might somehow be more coverage. It was unlikely, but it couldn't hurt. I asked him if they were handy. He went to get them, and returned with a fat manila envelope.

"Take them with you," he said.

I gave Watson my card and said I'd be in touch. As I was going out the door he laid a hand on my arm. "Mr. Duncavan . . ." His eyes were worried. "I've always tried to do the right thing, all my life, always tried to be righteous in the eyes of the Lord. I'm sorry that man got killed, powerful sorry for his family. But I didn't do nothin' wrong. All I done was try to keep a nice building." He was silent again, then he asked, "You think they goin' to take away my building?"

I almost gave him a legal opinion. I looked away. "We'll do everything we can," I said. But I didn't even know where to start.

Chapter Four

Back downtown I stopped at Monk's pub, ordered a double Stoli on the rocks at the bar. I'm not a drunk, or at least I don't think I am. They always say the drunk's the last to know. I never drink before lunch and generally my head's pretty clear when I wake up. On the other hand, I can't deny a frequent, powerful craving, and the rosy glow of my nose, those little spider veins in my Irish cheeks, don't come from healthy living.

I went to the phone booth, called my number, checked for messages on my answering machine (none), then carried the drink to an empty booth where I could spread out and think. I opened the envelope Watson gave me, sorted through the various papers, located the policy covering his building. The carrier was Heartland Indemnity. Watson had purchased it through an agency, Red Eagle Associates. I checked the declarations page: the coverage was one million dollars. I looked through the remaining papers on the slim possibility of some umbrella coverage, but there was nothing else.

I returned the papers to the envelope, sipped my Stoli, and asked myself the question: what the hell am I looking for? What could I dig up that would keep Moses Watson from losing his building? Admit it; you don't have a clue. If we could prove Bartodziec was a trespasser, that would do it. What if he was there to score drugs? That would defuse a lot of jury sympathy, but it didn't necessarily make him a trespasser, and you might not be able to get it into evidence. Anyway, my gut told me he wasn't there to score drugs, and with so little time, I had to rely heavily on my gut. I knew this: any straw that might offer Watson a chance to keep his building was out of reach until I could figure out what Bartodziec was doing there.

In this city of neighborhoods, the walls which divide one enclave from another are fortified each according to its own culture—snobbery, gangs, language, ethnicity, whatever. Bartodziec had crossed over something. If I could just find what bridged that crossing, it would mark the way like a road sign. The place of his death was as distant from his Polish community as Sparta was from Gary. Where was the touchstone between those worlds? What music had he heard, drifting over the wall?

I took out my notebook, turned to a blank page, started to sketch out a plan. The only way I could help Watson was to find out why Bartodziec died, and a good starting point would be to interview his close friends. But the best source of names would be the widow, and the rules of ethics put any contact with her strictly off limits.

I could, of course, go through formal channels. Artemus could serve an interrogatory on Hollis Lagatee requesting the names of the decedent's close associates. Lagatee would consult the widow, prepare formal answers, send them to her for signature, she'd return them, they'd be filed in court, and we'd get a copy. The rules gave them twenty-eight days to answer. There simply wasn't time. Besides, anyone disclosed that way would have been prepared by Lagatee long before I knocked on his door. Not that Hollis would tell them to lie. Hollis wasn't that kind of lawyer. But he would let them know that I did not have the best interests of the widow at heart. I could try finding Bartodziec's co-workers myself. Worth a try, though after five years, that trail would likely be frozen solid. I jotted down: Check cab company/machine shop for co-workers.

But before that I'd stop in to see Stanley Janda. Stan and I were law school buddies, along with Jack Merriweather— three policemen in law school at a time when policemen rarely went to college. Janda stayed on the police depart- ment after graduation, climbed through the ranks to be- come a Deputy Superintendent, then retired and opened a neighborhood law practice on Milwaukee Avenue. Merriweather became a justice of the appellate court. And then there's me. According to Joseph Campbell, some prim- itive tribe had a saying: "Look to where you stumble, for there you will find your fortune." I have stumbled so many times I should wear a helmet.

Janda grew up in Bartodziec's neighborhood, spoke Polish before he spoke English. As a lawyer he had no trouble making a niche there, even advertised on a Polish radio station. It was a tight little community. A long shot, but Janda still had a copper's instincts, and he just might know someone who knew Bartodziec. I wrote one word: Janda.

I turned to the page where I'd written down the names of Watson's five former tenants:

Robert Norton—1 North.	CTA bus driver.
Calvin Clark—2 South.	Deceased.
Booker Coleman—2 North.	Retired. Occupation unknown.
Mattie Croyance—3 South.	On Social Security, lived alone.
Fannie Walker—3 North.	Elderly domestic.

Fannie Walker was the one who'd called the police. Even if I found her, she probably couldn't tell me any more than she'd already told the detectives. But I still had to talk to her, have her tell me face-to-face what she remembered of that night. As far as finding any of the other tenants, the most promising might be Robert Norton, who worked for the CTA. Even if he was no longer working there, they might have a recent address. If he was retired, his file would probably show where they were sending his pension check. I made a note: Subpoena Norton's employment records. There wasn't time for the usual sort of subpoena, but I could try serving the subpoena personally, maybe get a look at the records first hand.

Then there was Shavonne Sykes, the missing witness, the supposed sometime-tenant who said she complained to Watson about the broken locks and crime in the building, to no avail. Who the hell was she, and where did Lagatee find her? She might even be easier to find than Norton, since we had her last known address. But at the moment, locating Lagatee's missing witness seemed to fall into the self-inflicted foot-wound category. If she never turned up, there was a good chance of the trial ending in a directed verdict for Watson. There was no point in handing Lagatee his star witness on a silver platter. But even though finding her seemed a bad idea, she was giving off an enticing scent. I had a hunch, with her suspicious disappearance, and the fact that Moses Watson never heard of her, that I could blow her story out of the water. She was almost certainly lying, but what was her motive, and who put her up to it? Not Lagatee. He wasn't that kind of lawyer, and he didn't need to be. Not the widow. She was too far removed from that neighborhood.

The place had emptied out, with only two tables occupied and no one at the bar, so I signaled the bartender for another Stoli, and while he was getting it, I wrote: Talk to Danny McGarry. As Watson's personal lawyer, McGarry might have a shred of something. Anything. The investigative leads were looking like a Christmas turkey four days afterward.

Besides, Danny was not only young and idealistic, he was a police fan to boot, and would probably make an enthusiastic ally. After he'd found out I was an ex-copper, he would prod me to talk about the police department. It made me uncomfortable at first; I didn't know if he knew I'd been fired. But he must have found out, because one day he asked me, right out of the blue, what it felt like to get shot. Anyone else, I would have told him to eat shit, but not Danny. He was too sincere, and he meant well. Once he asked me if I liked pistol shooting, told me he'd acquired a .45 Glock when he was with the Peace Corps in Somalia, but he wasn't very good with it. I told him how I used to shoot in matches with a .45 Gold Cup, how I'd handloaded my own ammo, but that had been a long time ago. The next day his law clerk dropped off a brown paper bag at my office, filled with about three hundred empty .45 casings. I put it in my basement, next to my dust-covered reloading equipment.

Danny joined the Peace Corps right out of law school, and was sent to Somalia as an advisor to law enforcement. To his credit, he knew that with no law enforcement experience he was completely unqualified; he described the whole experience as another high water mark in American arrogance. But he'd made the best of it, told me he would base his advice on what he'd seen on TV cop shows. I never knew if he was kidding, but it was a fact that Danny loved cop shows. Whenever I'd run into him, on the street or at the courthouse, he'd buttonhole me, ask me if I'd caught this or that episode of *Law & Order* or *NYPD Blue* or *Homicide*, did I think it was realistic. In a way, he was a big bear of a kid, and I'm afraid I disappointed him. I don't watch

TV cop shows. Even when I'm sitting alone in my living room, the sight of a bunch of pampered actors waving pistols around turns me purple with embarrassment. At Blockbuster, any video showing a movie star holding a gun gets an immediate pass.

I wanted to get a look at Watson's building, but decided to stop home first, grab some dinner, spend a little quality time with Stapler.

Chapter Five

I found a parking spot in front of the house, a two-story bungalow in Bucktown with green clapboard siding, one of those old frame buildings with a front door two steps below sidewalk level. My landlord, a retired fireman who's crazy about Stapler, lives on the first floor. Bucktown was an old neighborhood, but the gentrification onslaught was closing in; a Starbucks recently opened its doors around the corner, and it was only a matter of time before latte-sipping, briefcase-swinging yuppies crowded the sidewalks, and you wouldn't be able to find a parking space for all the SUVs. What do these people want?

I grabbed the mail from the top box and sorted through, hoping to find something more interesting than bills. No such luck. Stapler was insanely happy to see me, and I took him, leaping and whirling, out in the yard, spent a few minutes letting him retrieve his bumper. In practice he's a great bird dog. If he sees a sparrow in the back yard, he'll snap rock solid on point. Even in the field, he'll hold point on just about anything. Anything but game birds. Turtles, frogs, butterflies, animal bones—he looks like a model for Currier and Ives. Game birds, though, he just can't wait to make them fly away.

Actually, Stapler owes his name to Artemus Shumway, though Artemus has never seen the dog. Artemus is a fishing buddy, but he cannot stand the thought of shooting little birds out of the sky. I brought the puppy home after Beth and I split up, and three weeks later, I still had not thought of a name. Beth had been the imaginative one, the creative half of our broken partnership. In that insanity called mid-life crisis, I'd decided I no longer wanted to be married, was ecstatic with my new-found freedom. And I missed my wife terribly. I wanted freedom, I wanted to fornicate with strange women twice daily, then come home to my Beth. But Beth was gone. So the dog drove home with me from the kennel on the front seat of my shiny new, cherry-red Corvette.

When I told Artemus I was stuck for a name for the pup, he said: "Close your eyes; you're floating on a mountain lake. Smell the balsam, the crisp, clean air. First image comes to mind, that's the dog's name." I did, sitting at my desk. Somewhere from the inner reaches of my unconscious it came, rotating out of the blackness like a lost astronaut: the cantilevered form of my Bostitch.

After playing with Stapler for fifteen minutes, I zapped a Hungry Man dinner in the microwave, stood at the counter, and ate out of the container. Then I fed Stapler and found a flashlight in the kitchen drawer, but as I was leaving he gave me such a look of betrayal that I told him he could come. He did his manic routine again, whirling and dancing all the way to the car.

I took Armitage to Larabee, turned east on North Avenue. It was nearly dark when I turned onto Cleveland, one of those humid evenings when the air is like a blanket on your face. People sat on porches, stood in shadowy clusters along the sidewalk. I cruised slowly, managing to draw all eyes my way. Or at least it felt that way. Then I caught sight of Watson's building looming up in mid-block, plywood-covered windows glowing out of the dark stone like the eyes of a spider.

I found a parking space a few doors away and, wishing I'd brought a leash, told Stapler to heel. He fell in step with

47

me. When I reached the front entrance I saw why Watson had given me two keys. A chain link fence sealed off the front of the building, and the gate was padlocked. One of the keys slipped in easily, but would not turn. As I tried the other one I saw two young black men, lean, white tee shirts, approaching along the sidewalk. They were taking their sweet time, eyeing me. The second key did not seem to fit at all. I slipped the first one back into the cylinder plug. The two men stopped, standing too close, one on each side of me. Stapler wagged his tail. The key wouldn't work. I half-turned, vulnerable, made eye contact with the taller one.

"Yo," the tall one said. He was wearing a do-rag and missing a few teeth.

"Yo," I said.

"Whatcha doin', man?" he asked.

I mulled over some possibilities. Selling Bibles door to door. Trolling for muggers. Lick my dick. I said, "Trying to get the motherfucker to work."

"Jiggle it," he said.

"Yeah," the short one said. "Jiggle it. Sometimes they get rusty 'n shit, specially when they ole. Try jigglin' it."

I jiggled it. It worked. "Thanks," I said.

"Hey, no problem." They moved on.

The key in the front door worked easier. The hallway was pitch black and reeked of burnt wood, and I snapped on the flashlight, the tile floor gritty and crackling underfoot. Everything was black and charred; hard to believe the building was salvageable. I cast the flashlight beam up the open stairwell three stories, to a skylight half-covered with plywood. I started up the stairs, moving slowly, testing each tread. When I reached the second floor, I stepped into a broad hallway with a railing around the stairwell. This was where Bartodziec had been found, near the stairs. The fire damage was worse here.

Looking up to the third floor, you could see the door to Fannie Walker's apartment. If she had come out and looked over the rail, she would have had an unobstructed view of Bartodziec. Probably of his assailant, too. She probably could have witnessed the shooting. But she never opened the door. Or so she said. I walked around to the back of the staircase, played the beam along the underside of the stairs to the third floor. They looked pretty bad, the top two treads burned completely through. But I wanted to see exactly what view Mrs. Walker would have had, had she looked. I considered whether to chance it, then noticed Stapler wasn't with me. I called him. He didn't come. I whistled, then listened for movement from below. Nothing. I wasn't worried; it was no different than when we were hunting.

I decided to try it one step at a time. I started up, testing each stair, shifting my weight gradually as the tread took it. By the time I reached the third from the top I was confident; too confident. As I gave it my weight my foot broke through, and I grabbed for the banister, knocking the flashlight from my hand, sending it crashing to the floor below. It went out. I was in total darkness, clinging to the banister, and I felt something creak under my weight, felt the staircase shift. But the banister held. For what seemed like an hour I was afraid to move an eyelid. I hung on, in blackness like the inside of a grave, half-kneeling on the stair, leg hanging through the hole, one hand on the rail, the other gripping a baluster. Gradually I shifted my weight to my hands, then worked my leg free, found the next lower stair with my toe, eased my weight onto it. It felt solid and I stood tentatively, then lowered myself slowly back down until I reached the safety of the second floor.

I decided I didn't really care what Mrs. Walker would have seen. I found the railing with my hand and felt my way along it, sweeping ahead with one foot, searching for the flashlight. I must have groped along that way for two minutes when my toe struck the flashlight and it sputtered with a dim orange light. I picked it up, snapped the switch full on. It worked fine. I called the dog again, shined the light over the rail to the first floor, listened for movement somewhere. Nothing.

I went back down, probed all around the hallway with the beam, calling, "Stapler, come, boy." The doors to the apartments were closed, but I had left the front door open, and I went out to the front porch and called to him from there. At the edges of the light from the street lamps, dark faces turned in my direction. The gate in the cyclone fence was shut, and the dog was not in the enclosure. Now I was beginning to worry. Back inside, I noticed the basement door ajar, and I called down the stairs, again listening for a response. Nothing. I played the flashlight down the stairway. The basement seemed to have escaped damage from the fire, and I headed down, an odor of mildew mingling with the smell of charred wood.

To the right of the stairs was an open area draped in cobwebs, the back door at the far end. To the left a passageway led between gray plank doors, the ceiling above interlaced with forced air ducts. I followed the passageway to a back room, an old-fashioned boiler hunkering there, ducts streaming out of its head like a Medusa on steroids. Next to it was a kind of long wooden box made of coarse boards, which may have once held coal. Then I saw it, standing out of the narrow space between the box and the wall: the long, straight tail of Stapler on point. I moved behind him but he ignored me, mesmerized in whatever he was pointing at.

"Easy, fella," I said. As I touched his back he broke and whined, then scurried back, pressing himself, shaking, against my leg. I jabbed the flashlight beam into the space. It looked like a pile of old clothing. Then I noticed something odd at the far end, a crumpled gray suit that didn't seem quite empty. Looking closer, I saw it was worn by a skeleton lying across a pile of rags, poised as though at the bottom of a push-up, the skull looking over its shoulder, teeth like stained piano keys, empty eye sockets leering at me.

Chapter Six

It seemed misshapen somehow, a dwarf maybe. I left it there, not wanting to contaminate a crime scene, and went back upstairs, not sure who to call first. I knew I couldn't reach Artemus at this hour. From the front porch I dialed the police on my cell phone, then called Watson, knowing the cops would be on him like yellow jackets at an August picnic. He asked me if he should come over. I told him no, the cops knew where to find him, that I'd come by his place in a little while. I thought that if the cops were going to talk to him he should have a lawyer present, then with a twist in my belly I remembered: that wouldn't be me. I was not a lawyer—how long would it take that fact to reach all the crannies of my brain?

I waited on the front stoop, dreading the arrival of the beat car, remembering from my own days in homicide that the luckless bastard who found the body was always the first suspect. I just didn't need the aggravation.

Ten minutes later the whole street was dancing in blue and red strobes, the air full of the squawk and hiss of police radios. A crowd had gathered out front. I wanted to tell the cops to shut the lights off. I wanted to tell half of them to get the hell out of there, knowing most of them had nothing better to do, and were just plain nosy. I told the beat officer what I knew, asked him to snap the lock shut when he left. He told me to wait. I gave him my card, told him I had to go, knowing he'd tell me I had to wait for the detectives, knowing he'd imply I had no choice. Knowing I did, I drove over to Moses' place.

At ten o'clock I again found myself with Moses Watson. He sat quietly in his pajamas, arms across his knees, white head bowed.

"How often have you been to the building since the fire?" I asked him.

He looked over at the table lamp. "Once with the insurance people, then once when they put up the fence around the front door. That's it. I got no reason to go there." He looked back at the carpet, shook his head wearily, then spoke so softly I almost couldn't hear him. "I've always tried to be a righteous man, Mr. Duncavan."

"It's Mike. Look, it's really no big deal. So somebody dumped a body in your building. Mr. Watson—I don't want to knock your neighborhood, but you know yourself, homicide isn't exactly unknown there. You've done your best to secure the building. It's not your fault. It's got nothing to do with you." Actually that was only half-true. Abandoned buildings drew crime like a magnet draws iron filings. The city building department did everything it could to knock them down. Reacting to pressure from community groups, they had an aggressive tear-down program. If a building was vacant and not completely secured, it came down. A vacant building in that neighborhood stood like a wounded elephant on the veldt, bulldozers eyeing it by day, gangs circling by night. The cyclone fence around the front of Watson's building wasn't much protection.

"But how could they get in?" Moses was looking at me.

I shrugged. "Who else has keys?"

"No one. You're the only one. I only got two sets. I gave one to you."

"You've got it as secure as you can make it. Don't worry about it." I told him the detectives would probably be coming by that evening, and left.

At home I poured a hefty Stoli on the rocks, hoping to throw off that creeping sense of unworthiness hanging behind my shoulder like a corpse on a rope. I had fifteen days. I might as well have agreed to move the Rock of Gibraltar. I turned on the reading light next to my big chair, cracked open *The Confessions of St. Augustine*, Stapler's cold nose pressed to my bare ankle. Every now and then his flanks quivered in doggie dreams. After the fifth reading of one paragraph, I still had not escaped the verity that I had not a single clue, that I didn't know where to begin, and didn't even know what I was looking for. I put St. Augustine down, picked up instead an old Frederick Marryat novel I'd started two months ago. The characters' names were familiar, but who were they? I turned off the light and went to bed.

I did not dream at first. Then I dreamed of Beth, her hair short like she'd worn it in college, her brown eyes bright, her smile gladdening my heart. We were in a sitting room somewhere, a place I didn't recognize. A rectory? Waiting for someone to come, but I didn't know who. "You worry too much," she was saying. Then suddenly she was gone, and my heart plunged like a stalled airplane, knowing that I'd lost her, and I was sitting alone in that room, dreading the coming of that unknown person. My eyes snapped open, that trapped rodent fear gnawing at my belly, the sad early light spilling across the sheets. What is this thing which terrorizes me? Well, who else is here, kiddo, who else gives a shit? We are all the embodiment of our own pathos. Just not pathetic enough to be interesting. If this be self-pity, let's have a look. Examine thyself, trace the bell-shaped curve of your wretched life. What is there that you have not yet failed at? Artemus Shumway takes pity, hands you this sinecure, this mirror which you will hold up in the end to examine one more failure.

Tuesday, August 8

I tried to go back to sleep, started drifting back into that nether twilight, and was jarred by the memory of the eardrum blast of gunshots, those sudden muzzle flashes, the lance of pain through my ankle. I got up, pulled on shorts and an Adidas tee shirt.

Outside in the cool dawn, I unlocked my bicycle. Before I'd taken a bullet through the ankle, running had been part of my regimen. Now it's just the bike. I set off for no particular destination, then remembered that I'd left it to the cops to lock up Watson's building the night before, and turned in that direction. It was about four miles away, with almost no traffic. I took Armitage to Clybourn to North. After turning into Watson's block, deserted at this hour, I found the padlock on the gate snapped shut, the front door closed. Not having the keys with me, I walked the bike around the back, leaned it against the fence, and descended the stairs to the basement door looking for some breach, some place that intruders could have gotten in. The stairway was cool, the area outside the door had a sour, dank smell. The basement door was new, rock-solid, and locked. I climbed the open back stairway to the top, checking the back doors to the second and third floors. The whole building seemed tight as a drum. I could not understand how anyone would get in without a key; without breaking and entering. I turned my bike homeward, traffic beginning to thicken, the heat already rising. By the time I reached home my tee shirt was dripping wet.

I worked out on the light bag for awhile, then punched

the heavy one, thinking all the while there was some connection between the murder and the breach of security at Watson's building. Logically it made no sense, of course; maybe, with nothing to go on, I was kidding myself. But it was there in my gut, and it would be unwise to ignore it.

I showered, my dream of Beth working back into my head like smoke. I ached for her. We'd been college sweethearts; she was six years younger. She quit school to marry me, shortly after I started with the police department, stood by me through those night school years, even forgave me that one spectacular breach of fidelity, which had been marked by gunshots, newspaper stories, death, and disgrace.

In a world where truth becomes ever more elusive, one thing seemed immutable: Beth was the best thing that ever happened to me. A Catholic girl in the best sense, she shouldered the public embarrassment, forgave my unfaithfulness. But when it came to the game of infidelity, I had season tickets; she would not forgive the whole series. Only because of her unyielding charity, the divorce was amicable. I took her Omni, gladly gave her my new Lexus. Hard to believe, looking back, but at that moment I felt liberated. Free to chase a whole world full of pussy without regret. Beth even said that, in the eyes of God, she felt she was still married to me. She never did marry again. Not yet, anyway. I still see her now and then, drive out to Sutler's Grove on a Saturday morning. She always seems glad to see me.

Beth found success the way I found failure, turning a hobby, the sculpting of bronze statuettes, into a flourishing enterprise. After the divorce, she bought an old house in Sutler's Grove, an artist's community sixty miles northwest of Chicago, and converted the small barn into a studio. She turns out limited edition figurines, much of it outdoors stuff, hunting dogs and flying ducks, moose and deer and bears. There's even one of Stapler on point. But her most popular pieces are bronze children, frozen Norman Rockwell moments. Little boys shooting marbles, little girls whispering to each other on back steps. She works alone and is always busy, at ease on the favorable side of supply and demand, commanding large prices for her "collectibles."

I fed Stapler and let him out in the yard. It was still early, but I dialed Moses' number, wanting to know how it went the night before. He picked up on the second ring.

"How'd it go with the police last night?" I asked.

"Police never came by," he said.

At first I thought I misunderstood. "Never came by? You're sure?" It was a stupid, condescending question. Covering, I didn't wait for an answer. "I'm just really surprised." And then I did it again. "You're sure?" Maybe he was asleep, didn't hear the doorbell.

"I stayed awake most of the night. Even slept on the couch in the living room. Nobody came by."

I thanked him, told him I'd be in touch. Puzzled, I dialed Area One Violent Crimes. The shift would just be changing from the midnight to day watch, though the detectives who handled it were probably working the afternoon shift and wouldn't be there. The detective who answered gave his name but I didn't catch it.

"I'm calling about a homicide that was reported last night, on Cleveland," I said.

"Who are you?"

"I'm the guy who found the body."

"Hold on," he said, and put the phone down. He came back a minute later. "There were no homicides last night."

That stopped me. Then I realized, he probably thought I

was talking about a fresh murder. "Look, I'm sorry, I should have explained. It was a skeleton, in a vacant building on Cleveland." They certainly wouldn't classify it as a homicide without knowing a cause of death.

"No, if they found a skeleton, it would have been logged in. We had nothing like that last night."

"Look, I'm the guy who found it. The police were there."

He took a second. "Did you get the name of the detective assigned?"

"No, I didn't hang around."

"You *left?*" Now he seemed exasperated. "So what do you want?"

"Look, this is important. I represent the building owner in some litigation. I couldn't hang around last night, but I left my card. I want to cooperate."

He thought another minute. "You're a lawyer?" Then without giving me a chance to answer he said, "Okay, listen, I just walked in when you called—" I could hear someone talking to him. "Hang on a minute." He put his hand over the mouthpiece, and there was a muffled conversation I couldn't make out. Then I was sure someone distinctly uttered the words "whale penis." There was a short burst of laughter, and he came back. "I'm going to put you on hold a second. The sergeant wants to talk to you."

A minute passed. They didn't even play music. "This is Sergeant Galanopoulos," someone said finally. "You the guy found the skeleton last night?"

I was pretty sure that was what I told the first guy, twice. I was beginning to get steamed. "Yeah," I said.

"You're, um, the private eye?" He seemed amused. "Some kind of a sleuth guy, like in the movies?" Someone guffawed in the background.

58

It was too early to put up with this shit. "Look, is this your dim-witted way of making a point?"

"Wait now, don't get all testy. Play your cards right, I put you in for a junior policeman's badge."

"Listen, douche bag, I know your commander. Now you gonna tell me what the fuck's going on, or do I call him?" I was going too far. I did know his commander. His commander didn't like me.

"Whoa, all right, now listen, here's the deal. That case was way out of our league, see, so we turned it over to the, ah, monkey squad." Roar of laughter in the background. "See, the skeleton you found—it happens to be a gorilla."

I didn't say anything for several seconds, trying to get my brain to compute.

"You still there?" he asked.

After hanging up I sat a minute, wishing I'd been smart enough to have taken a closer look at the skeleton. Then, still stung, I got Stapler in from the yard, took a leash this time, and drove to Watson's building. I went straight to the basement. The high windows shed only meager daylight. In the furnace room I turned on the flashlight, played it around behind the furnace. The skeleton was gone, of course, but now I noticed a smell forcing itself above the mustiness, something that had reached only the borders of my consciousness last night: jasmine. I couldn't tell where it was coming from. There were old boxes scattered along the walls, but the center of the floor seemed clean. Too clean. Something else I failed to notice last night—the floor had recently been swept. This time I decided to take my time, go over the whole basement like a crime scene.

I made a rough sketch of the floor plan, then made a preliminary check of the other rooms, small cubicles which must have been used by tenants for storage. The rooms were largely empty, covered in a thin layer of dust. At the door of each I held the flashlight low, spreading the beam across the floor. Then in one I found something; small, bare feet had left prints in the dust. They crossed to a wooden chest in the corner. I measured the footprints against my pen, jotted some notes, and eyeballed the box. This wasn't a crime scene, no reason not to open it. Stapler brushing past me then, as interested in the chest as I was, sniffed all around it, along the closed lid, put his paws up and sniffed the top. But he didn't point, thank the Lord for small favors, and eventually lost interest. He wandered back out the door. The scent of jasmine was strong in here. I sniffed along the edge of the box myself. The smell was coming from inside. I opened it.

Stacked in one corner were bundles of jasmine incense sticks. There were satin garments of some kind, strange, colorful, hooded. I pulled them out, uncovering a pile of burnt candles and fat pieces of colored chalk. And the steely glint of three butcher knives. Using a handkerchief I picked them up gingerly by the wooden handles, one by one. The blades were clean. I put them back, replaced the way I'd found them.

Back in the boiler room, light from the windows oozed only dimly onto the floor. I snapped off the flashlight, let my eyes adjust, trying an examination without the stark contrast of the flashlight beam. After a minute I noticed something irregular on the surface of the floor and ran my fingers across it. Candle wax. I searched the entire floor then, found four other spots exactly the same, evenly spaced. If you connected the spots with chalk you'd have a pentagon; connect them a little more elaborately, it could be a pentagram.

Stapler whined. I turned, saw his ears pricked, eyes fixed

back toward the stairs to the first floor. He whined again, did a little tap dance. I thought I heard a soft footfall upstairs. Imagination? Then he started barking in earnest and I grabbed his collar, sure now I heard the upstairs vestibule door close. I started for the steps, changed my mind, went to one of the high windows at the front of the basement, rubbed a spot out of the grime with the side of my hand. I couldn't see much more than a corner of the front stoop, my car parked at the curb, and part of a blue Buick parked in front of it. An engine started. The Buick pulled away.

I trotted to the stairs and up to the first floor, checked the front door. It was locked, just as I'd left it. I went out the front door. There was a young man, about twenty-five, in a white undershirt, sitting on a porch across the street, watching me. I put Stapler on his leash and walked over. Close up, I saw it was one of the young men who'd stopped to talk to me last night. I tried a warm smile. He smiled back. "Nice lookin' dog," he said.

I nodded. Stapler gave him a friendly grin, wagged his tail.

"I'm wondering if maybe you could help me. I'm a friend of Moses Watson. Do you know him?"

"Old guy owns that building? Yeah. Know who he is."

"Did you see, ah, someone go into that building just now?"

"Sides you? Yeah, it was a lady."

"Do you know who she was?"

His expression turned wary. He shook his head. I could try for sympathy, bring up Watson's troubles, but decided to play it straight, at least sort of.

"Look, I'm a private investigator, I'm working for Mr. Watson. I want to thank you for helping me out last night, you and your friend. With the lock, I mean." His expression didn't change. "I wonder if you could help me some more, just answer a few questions. Of course I'll pay you for your time."

A smile popped into his face. "I be your man."

"The lady in the Buick. Ever see her before?"

He held out his palm. I fished a ten out of my wallet, handed it to him.

"No, I never seen her before, least I don't think so." He slipped the ten into his jeans pocket, returned his elbows to his knees. "She's not too bad looking, kinda skinny, dark-skinned sister. 'Bout thirty-five, I'd say."

"Ever see any, ah, unusual activity around the building? People going in and out?"

He looked down, traced a pattern on the step with his finger. I waited. He didn't look up. "Man, they's some kinda crazy shit goin' down in that building. All kind of weird shit."

"What kind of weird shit?"

He reflected a moment, then his response was almost defensive. "Voodoo shit. Devil shit."

"How do you know that?"

He shrugged. "Talk." He shrugged again. "Everybody in the neighborhood know it. Man, I don't want nothin' to do with that shit."

"Did you ever see anything?"

"One night, I see 'em goin' in there, real late. Pulled up in a rusty-ass old station wagon. Four of 'em, two ladies and two mans."

"Black folks?"

"Uh-huh."

"How'd they get in?"

He looked at me like I was silly. "The front door, like you. With a key."

"Did you recognize any of them?"

"I don't know those people. But I can tell you this much. They had a goat."

"A goat?"

"Yeah, a goat. They went in with a goat, but they sure's shit didn't come out with no goat. Man, whatever they be doin', I don't want nothin' to do with that shit."

"How long were they in there?"

"Hour, maybe two."

"Do you know what they were doing?"

He shook his head, but when I dug in my wallet and came up with another ten, he reconsidered. "Well . . . I went over there, tried to see in the basement window, but I couldn't see nothin.' I know they was lightin' candles, though. And singin' some kinda weird way. And beatin' a drum."

"The lady you saw today, was she one of them?"

"Can't rightly say. I told you, I don't know those people."

I thanked him, pulled out a card, jotted my home phone on the back, handed it to him. "I'm Mike Duncavan. Listen, you ever see anyone go in there again, call me, okay? Any time. I'll make it worth your while. You call me, all right?"

His friendly smile returned. "Name's Errol Flynn," he said, shaking my hand. "Like the movie star. Hey, don't worry, man, I see anything, I call you." He slipped the card into his pocket.

As I drove to the office I called Watson on my cell phone, told him about the ape skeleton, feeling pretty sheepish. If he thought I was a damn fool, he didn't let on. He seemed relieved, as though he had just gained a reprieve

63

from the bulldozers eyeing his building. He was truly puzzled, though. Then I told him about the wooden chest I'd found in the basement, asked again if anyone else had keys. No; he was positive. He had no idea who the chest belonged to, knew nothing about the activities the young man had described.

I hung up and, waiting at a very long light, I tried to put it together. The goat must have been sacrificed in the basement, which would explain the butcher knives in the trunk. But what about the ape? Where would they get it? The light turned green. I decided to put it out of my mind, to stay focused on finding out why Bartodziec was in the building the night he was killed. Maybe his murder was connected, somehow, to all this hocus pocus, but I had, what, fourteen days left?

Later that afternoon I walked over to Kinko's with a snapshot of Bartodziec I'd taken from the file, had four laser copies made. I paper-clipped a ten to the back of one, put it in my shirt pocket, and drove over to the cab company garage where Bartodziec had worked part-time. The dispatcher sat in a cubicle behind glass, with a round hole in the middle. I explained that I was investigating the death of a cab driver, asked him if he remembered Bartodziec. He looked at me warily, shook his head. When I told him he'd worked there five years ago, he guffawed. "You got any idea how many types of foreigners come and go in this place?" he said. "You must be fuckin' silly."

In those dull eyes I could see that as a kid, he'd probably eaten a lot of paint chips. I was beginning to understand why he needed to be behind bullet-proof glass. I took a breath, pleased with myself, since a number of years ago I would have walked around, kicked in the door, and squeezed his throat until his eyes popped. I used to take pride in that, being able to choke a dirtbag with one hand. But even if I were so inclined, I wasn't sure I could still do it.

He leaned forward, stage-whispered, "What was he? We got every kind of towel head and sand nigger there is."

I was also beginning to understand why he had not chosen a career path in, say, diplomacy. Or maybe he knew an Arab named Tadeusz Bartodziec. I slid the photograph through the opening, and as he studied it, he slipped the ten from under the paper clip and into his pants' pocket with the dexterity of a stage magician. He shook his head, started to hand it back.

"Tell you what," I said. "Keep it, show it around."

He grinned wickedly, showing brown teeth, letting me know he was not the kind of guy you put things over on. "Wait a minute. Why should I help you?"

"You get a twenty for anyone you find who knew him."

His smile turned to a frown and he nodded slowly, letting me know it was not without qualms that he surrendered to the forces of darkness. "Okay, then," he said.

Chapter Seven

I drove back to the Loop thinking the cab company was probably a dead end. Bartodziec worked there only part-time and too long ago, and I had a feeling it was not a place where fast friendships developed. Leads would have to come from elsewhere.

At my desk I spun the Rolodex, found two numbers: Stanley Janda and Danny McGarry. I reached Janda right away. When I told him I needed to talk to him he asked no questions, said he was waiting for a client to show up for an appointment, but I could come by about one-thirty. I told him I'd be there, was about to dial McGarry's number when the phone rang. It was McGarry.

"Moses Watson called me," he said, "told me you'd been by to see him. Nice we're on the same side for a change, Mike. I thought it was super when Artemus Shumway finally took over the case. Now with you on board—geez, Moses can't lose!"

"I was just going to call you. We need to talk," I said.

"Why don't you come by now?"

"See you in half an hour."

He started to hang up. "Oh, Mike. Did you know I've moved?" He gave me his new address, a much fancier building. Also a longer walk.

I made my way along the crowded lunch hour sidewalks wondering, as I often had, how Danny was able to make any money with all his volunteerism. At the Bar Association, he was forever caught up in some well-intentioned but naive pro bono program. Occasionally he'd tried to get me involved, but feeling guilty, I always demurred. Now it seemed Danny was doing pretty well. It was nice to see virtue rewarded.

By the time I punched the elevator button for his floor, my ankle was killing me, and as I approached his receptionist, I made a conscious effort not to limp. The office decor was pricey: oil paintings and expensive furniture. When Danny came out and greeted me, I almost didn't recognize him. His beer gut had disappeared, his cheeks, once rosy, looked drawn, and when he shook my hand he seemed somehow less jovial. With his baby fat gone, he didn't look jolly any more. But I'd always looked at Danny as a big kid, and he wasn't.

He shut his office door behind us and stage-whispered, "You packing heat?" He actually said those words: "packing heat." Now I saw the Danny I knew: eternal adolescent.

I shook my head, moving to the view from his window. "I only wear a gun when I'm poking around Indian country," I said, looking over the green expanse of Grant Park, the rows of sailboats bobbing at anchor in the harbor. "You've got a great view."

"You really like it? Things are finally coming together for me, Mike."

"It's nice to see enterprise rewarded, Danny." He'd been a partner in a general practice firm, decided to strike out on his own.

"Well, it's paying off now, and no partners to worry about. I just settled a quad case." Meaning quadriplegic, the jackpot of personal injury cases. As the saying goes, it's cheaper to kill the plaintiff than to permanently cripple him. I hid my surprise. Danny's cases had always been the whiplash sort. With good liability, he was talking millions of dollars, of which the lawyers take a third. A major settlement like that usually starts a buzz up and down LaSalle Street, though, and I hadn't heard a thing. Another sign, I guessed, that I was out of the Loop in more ways than one.

"You still doing all that pro bono work?" I asked.

"I've cut way back. Still taking a case now and then for New Horizons. You know that organization?"

I shook my head.

"They investigate racial discrimination in apartment leasing. If there's been a suspicious refusal to rent an apartment to a minority, they send checkers to apply. When they get a clear-cut case, I'll file a civil rights action. The evidence is usually pretty compelling, so they almost always settle."

"Still single?" I asked.

He smiled, shook his head. "I guess it has been awhile since we've talked. Married and divorced. Didn't last long." Now it was his turn to change the subject. "I just bought a new house in Barrington. You've got to come out and see it, Mike. It's so cool, my neighbors have horses. Beautiful, they come right up to my fence. I've got a really neat pool— and hey, I've got a pistol range in the basement. Well, not really a range, but I got a bullet trap down there. Basement's fifty feet long. Come out, we can shoot, go for a swim."

"Danny, I haven't shot a pistol in years. I still have all that .45 brass you gave me."

"All the better. Listen, I challenge you to a match, Mike. Loser buys dinner. How about this Saturday?"

I gathered he was lonely, rattling around in that big house. I looked at my watch. "Listen, Danny, I got to run soon, and we need to talk about Moses Watson."

"Sure." he leaned back in his chair, crossed his arms. "Situation's kind of a Catch-22. City wants the building torn down, we're trying to get the money to fix it up, but the insurance company's dragging its heels. I think they think it was an arson." Danny chuckled. "Can you see Moses torching his own building?"

"I never heard of the insurance agency. Red Eagle? Moses said you got the insurance for him."

"He what?" Danny grinned, shook his head. "No, Mike. Moses says things, sometimes . . ." His voice trailed off. "I worry about him. I really think he's starting to lose it. Some days he's sharp as a tack, and others?" He shook his head again. "He tried to find a mortgage, so he could start the work. Right now the building's free and clear, but he still couldn't find a lender to do it, not in that neighborhood. And even with a mortgage, the building wouldn't start paying off for awhile, when it's occupied and rents start coming in. I'm afraid without immediate income, Moses couldn't carry the paper."

I told Danny then about the chest I found in the basement, the candle wax on the floor, the comings and goings late at night. I also told him I'd found some "animal bones," neglecting the part about reporting the skeleton to the police. "Did anyone else have access to the building?" I asked.

He knotted his brow. "Don't think so. God knows, I've warned Moses to be real careful about giving anyone the keys. Far as I know, he's got just the one set. But hey, that's some weird shit, isn't it? Any idea what that's all about?"

I told him I didn't have a clue, which seemed the cosmic truth of the hour.

"Mike, there's another problem with the insurance company. Moses thought he was insured for replacement cost, but he's not. He's trying to say the agent told him he was, but that wasn't in the declarations. It's one more complication holding up the settlement. But I think I'm making some headway."

"Have you thought of filing a declaratory judgment action against the insurance company?"

"I filed a suit for breach of contract. It's coming up for a case management conference with the judge this week. I should have filed a DJ, I guess, but insurance litigation is a little out of my league."

"There's no heavy lifting. Most DJs get resolved on summary judgment, and at least you're putting the insurance company on the defensive. Why don't you amend your complaint, add a count for declaratory judgment, and another one for bad faith."

"Thanks, I'll try that. We'd better make some headway in the next six weeks. I've bought about as much time as I can in housing court. Otherwise they're going to flatten the building and send Moses the bill for demolition. Mike, I'm afraid he's slipping. Seems to have good days and bad days. Sometimes he's normal as you and me, other times . . ."

"Anything you can tell me about the shooting?"

Danny shrugged his shoulders. "I've handled his building violations, that's about it. You probably know more than I do."

I got up, thanked him, headed for the door.

"How about next Saturday, coming by the house?"

"I'll have to call you, Danny," I said. "I got to check my calendar."

Chapter Eight

It was too early to drive out to meet Stanley Janda. I walked back to my office, and in a deep funk I sat down, spun my chair to face the window to watch the foot traffic streaming below. With less than fourteen days before discovery closed, I had no leads, didn't even know where I was going. I could call the detectives who investigated Bartodziec's murder, but after five years they wouldn't remember anything they hadn't included in their reports. The file was lying there on my desk, and to get the best of inertia, I pulled out the case report. The detective was Andrew Bertucci, Area Five Violent Crimes. I found the number in my own directory and dialed, hoping Bertucci would still be assigned there, five years later, but he wasn't. The detective who answered thought Bertucci had been transferred to Area Three. I tried there; the sergeant who answered said Bertucci was on the street. I explained that I needed to talk to him about a civil case that was going to trial. He was pleasant, said he'd call the dispatcher, have Bertucci call me.

I hung up dispirited, again turned to the pedestrian traffic beneath my window, and suddenly there appeared a vision. Heading my way, curved hips swaying in a narrow black skirt, a sublime set of hooters bouncing in a scoop-necked ivory blouse, a waterfall of blonde hair spilling over her shoulders. And God created Woman! She crossed Washington, studying something in her hand. She turned east, stopped below my window to wait for the light, still rapt in what I could now see was a note. Then she looked up and I thought she saw me, but her eyes were looking inward—she seemed to be crying. The light changed and she tore the note into little pieces, threw them on the sidewalk, and stalked across Wells Street.

I watched those bits of paper disappearing beneath the feet of an oblivious humanity. What kind of message had brought such ache to a young heart? What turning point did it mark in her gorgeous life? Was I the only curious soul in the whole world? A break came in the passing foot traffic, and the pieces were still there, rearranging themselves like fat snowflakes in a puff of wind.

Possessed by a need to know what was in that note, I ran out the door and down the stairs, and when I reached the sidewalk I stepped into the passing crowd, trying to be cool. "Excuse me, sorry," retrieving the bits as the crowd stepped around me. I got all but three pieces, which had blown into the street. I snatched up two of them quickly, but the third eluded me, skittering through traffic. The light went red, the cars stopped, and I got to my hands and knees, spotted the last scrap under a car. I flopped onto my belly, slithered under, snatched it, and slid back out, waving and smiling at the cars behind—everything's all right, folks, I'm really perfectly sane. If someone had asked me at that moment, how the hell could you do that, all I could say is, how the hell could I *not* do that? It's usually easier to give in to my obsessions. If I could afford therapy, I'd get it.

I stuffed the torn pieces into my suit coat pocket, and when I got back to the office the phone was ringing. It was Detective Bertucci. I thanked him for calling back so promptly, told him I was investigating a civil lawsuit involving a murder. "Happened about five years ago, near Cabrini-Green—"

He interrupted. "Five years ago? Cabrini-Green?" He chuckled. "Sorry, but I doubt I'd remember anything that far back. Do you have copies of the case reports?"

"Yeah, but I wanted to talk to you anyway, if you don't mind."

"I don't mind, it's just that . . . do you know how many murders there's been in Cabrini-Green in the last five years?"

"Right, but this one was a little different, maybe it'll stand out. It didn't happen in the projects, it was nearby, in a six-flat. Polish guy, found shot in an apartment building hallway, still had his money in his wallet."

"Wait a minute." In the silence, I could sense lights coming on. "Yeah, I remember that one. Real clean building, right? We never did clear it. You're working for who, the widow?"

"No, the landlord. You said it was a real clean building?"

"Right, I mean, that's one of the reasons I remember it. I couldn't believe there was such a nice building over there. Neighborhood's a shit hole. Mostly it's been torn down now, but I remember that building, nice carpet on the stairs, mail boxes all intact. Real unusual, in that neighborhood. The victim was a white guy, Polish. I remember his wife didn't speak any English, and no one knew why he was in the building. We had no kind of leads. Zero. Probably still a mystery."

"Look, I'd like to drop by, talk about it some time."

"You're welcome to come by the station if you want, but I can tell you right now, everything I know is in my reports," he said.

"I'd still like to meet with you. At your convenience, of course."

"Sure. I'm working days, just give me a call when you want to come by. If I'm on the street, tell whoever answers to call the dispatcher. I'll come in and meet you."

Bertucci seemed like a good guy, and I was tempted to play do-you-know-so-and-so, but decided against it. It had been a long time since I carried a badge.

I hung up, wondering if he'd given up on the Bartodziec case before he started, had simply gone through the motions. The public has no idea how homicide investigation really works. It's not like television. It is anything but exciting or glamorous. In the O.J. Simpson case, the detectives were judged by a public whose only frame of reference was what they'd seen on TV, and they did not fare well. The trial itself became just another TV spectacular. But though the forensic dog and pony show has popular appeal, any seasoned detective knows that murders aren't solved by forensics. Forensics are important, but secondary.

Murders are solved by boring, tedious work, knocking on lots of doors, talking to lots of people. By trusting your hunches, following them relentlessly. And by playing a few psychological games. You bank on the fact that the victim and the killer are connected. You bank on the fact that someone must have seen or heard something. You bank on the fact that the bad guy will tell someone about it—he can't help himself. It's the old cliché: not even a fish would get caught if he kept his mouth shut. But a murderer can never keep his mouth shut after killing someone, it's just too big a deal. Your job is to find someone he told, and persuade that person to tell *you*.

Those are skills far removed from the crime lab. And when you've zeroed in, when you smell blood, you use the same skill to make the bad guy want to tell you all about it, too, every minuscule, insignificant detail. All's fair, so long as what you get is reliable. Which is why beating the shit out of a suspect is not a good idea. Tempting, sometimes, true. But murderers aren't always such bad people. In that slimy netherland where Bertucci does his work, killers sometimes make the world a better place for the rest of us. There were times I even thought of murder as one of the helping professions. A sort of community social work.

But in finding someone who knows something, the most fruitful fishing comes in finding, first, the connection between victim and killer. Usually you know right away. When you don't, that connection is the first thing to look for. When you can't find the connection, it's a very tough game. That's why serial killers, who have no link to the victim, go free for so long. With robberies gone bad, you've got the same problem. But whoever killed Bartodziec, robbery wasn't his motive. The killer left him to die in that hallway with money still in his pocket.

I wondered if Bartodziec's non-connection to that neighborhood, to those circumstances, might have put Bertucci off. There was no shortage of homicides in need of solving; sometimes you just have to move on to the next one.

I drove over to see Stan Janda. He had a neighborhood practice, with an office in a storefront on Milwaukee Avenue. My father used to say, "Ask a Polish person how to get to anywhere in the world and he'll tell you, 'First, you take the Milwaukee Avenue Bus . . .' " It was true, though: for the Polish in Chicago, the world seemed to begin and end on Milwaukee Avenue.

I found a parking space and walked to Janda's office, taking in the store windows, thinking that this street could be in any city in Poland. Polish was the language of the shop windows, of the people along the sidewalk. There were white ducks hanging upside down at the butcher shop, and a gift store window crowded with dolls in Polish costume, painted goose eggs, crystal vases etched with the visage of

Pope John Paul II. People seemed to be eyeing me. It wasn't my imagination—some would stop talking as I passed. I wondered what marked me as an outsider; I wasn't exactly dressed for the cover of *GQ*. Anyone who saw me park the Omni would not necessarily have been overcome with envy.

Janda's office was located on a busy corner, "ADWOCAT" printed in huge letters facing each street. In that precise Polish accent I find irresistible, a blonde receptionist said Janda would be out in a minute, asked me to take a seat. The office appeared utilitarian: metal desks, the basic machinery of a law practice, not much in the way of decor.

Stan, big, round-shouldered, with a Jay Leno jaw, came out to the waiting room and squeezed my shoulder as he shook my hand, giving me that Look of Concern. "How you making out, old buddy?"

"Knocking 'em dead," I said.

"I been thinking," he said as we walked back to his office, "I don't know if helping out a criminal lawyer is beneath you, but I could use a good investigator from time to time."

"Call me if you need me," I said.

"You mean you'd really stoop to that?" It was a reference to my law school resolve never to be a criminal lawyer.

"Stan, you'd be surprised what I'd stoop to." We sat down in his office. I asked how his practice was going.

"It's really good, almost all of my work comes from the Polish community. These are good folks, Mike, strong ethical values. They like to have a good time, maybe drink a little too much. DUIs pay the rent, I'm sorry to say. But they're simple people, in the best sense of the word—very trusting. I can't help thinking they're what Americans were like back during the war years."

"Trusting? You should have seen the suspicious looks I got as I walked over here."

He smiled. "No, by trusting I mean they're a little naive when it comes to business, they tend to assume everybody acts honorably. They're not good at paying attention to the fine print." He laughed. "And too cheap to hire a lawyer until they need one real bad." He sat back, laced his fingers across his stomach. "Sometimes I think the only thing that saves them from every con in the book is that they don't like to part with a nickel. They're suspicious of government, police, too. That's what you saw—you still look like a copper, you know that? Anyway, part of it's because of the regime they left behind in Poland, but you've got to remember, too, a lot of these people are illegals. They come over on a temporary visa and stay. A father will come over, work his ass off for a year, then bring an elder son over, then the two of them work to bring another, and so on. Sometimes the old man comes over, finds some sweet chickie, and forgets the rest."

I wanted to steer the conversation to the reason I came, and finally just said, "The dead guy's name was Tadeusz Bartodziec. I'm wondering if you've ever heard of him, or could maybe ask around if anyone knew him."

His answer surprised me. "I knew Tadeusz, yeah. This is a tight little community, everybody knows everybody else. For awhile my practice was about the only game in town. I did the immigration work for Tadeusz's family, a few other things."

I wondered why Mrs. Bartodziec didn't bring him the wrongful death case, but didn't know how to bring it up. "Mind telling me what kind of other things?"

He hesitated. "I guess I'm not breaking any confidences,

it's a matter of public record. They bought a small bun-galow on Wolfram, right around the corner from here. I handled the closing." He hesitated again. "A couple of criminal matters." He saw my sudden interest and smiled, shaking his head. "Nothing serious, a few minor scrapes. Tadeusz was a really good guy, but he was kind of—he had a short fuse. Everything was a matter of honor with him. He'd get offended, punch someone out, get himself locked up. Then he'd call me, full of remorse." Our eyes met and he laughed; pretty sure where this was going, I squirmed. "Like a good friend of mine I won't mention," he con-tinued. "Tadeusz never punched out a judge, though."

Actually, I was kind of relieved he'd brought it up, aired out that particular closet. Stan was probably the first person who'd ever raised the subject with me. "Except I don't have any remorse," I said.

"Sure you do," he said, and laughed again.

There was a lull in the conversation, and I decided just to ask him. "Any idea why the widow didn't bring the case to you? You were their lawyer, weren't you?"

He shrugged. "I see her on the street, she nods and smiles. You know yourself, there're too many lawyers chasing too few dollars." He turned to the window. "See that?" He pointed to a clothing store across the street, a blaze orange poster with black letters pasted up in one of the windows: NOTARY PUBLIC. "In Europe, a notary's a big deal, they do all sorts of things that only lawyers do here. I hear that guy over there is writing wills, doing God knows what else. But I can't prove it. Guys like him prey on the frugality of these people, tell them they don't need a lawyer. A lot of them bird-dog personal injury cases for am-bulance chasers, take a cut of the fee."

But he couldn't have been talking about this case. This

was Hollis Lagatee's case. Even if Hollis weren't Mr. Straightlaced, he'd never risk splitting a fee with a non-lawyer. You can get disbarred for that. Almost as fast as for punching out a judge. "Do you know if Tadeusz had any close friends?" I asked. "It's a long shot, but maybe someone would know what he was up to."

"I'll see what I can come up with, Mike. I know a guy Tadeusz worked with, I think they were pretty close. And know what? He owes me."

I wasn't comfortable with that. "Listen, Stan, I don't want you calling in any markers . . ."

He raised a hand. "No, no, I'm glad to do it. I'll ask him if he'll talk to you. But if he won't, that's up to him. I'll give him a call right now."

"Want me to step out?"

"Probably better."

I sat out in the waiting area, watching people drift past the windows, struck by a memory of Ashland Avenue on the south side, my old neighborhood. Storefronts just like these. Saturday afternoons—before the waxing of my boxing career—my mother took me shopping with her, to the bakery, the butcher shop, the greengrocer. She'd drive me nuts, stopping every fifty feet to chat with neighbors, people with whom she'd gone to St. Raphael's grammar school, whose children now went to St. Raphael's with me. As a kid in that neighborhood, you had to be careful what you did, knowing someone would surely tell your folks.

I looked over at the receptionist, caught her staring at me. She blushed, looked down at her work.

"Do you live in the neighborhood?" I asked.

She looked up and smiled. She had immaculate teeth. "I wouldn't live anywhere else."

"I used to live in a neighborhood just like this. South

side. Lots of Polish people there, too. Kind of a melting pot."

"I'm afraid it's changing, with the Spanish moving in . . ." She caught herself. "I don't mean the Spanish people. The gangs, though, Latin Kings—you've got to be so careful now, you can't even walk at night."

Stan appeared in the hallway then, waved me back to his office.

"The lady says you've got some gang problems in the neighborhood," I said. Stan had been one of the originals forming the Gang Crimes unit.

He nodded. "Yeah. We've had a rash of street robberies, mainly after dark." Standing behind his desk, he scribbled something on the back of his business card and handed it to me. "Florian Janicki, that's his home number. I talked to him at work." Judging from his upbeat tone, it must have gone well. "He's a foreman at a metal castings plant on Foster Avenue, but he works a second job in the evenings. He said he'll meet you Wednesday night at Wanda's, seven-thirty. It's a bar just up the street, past the big butcher shop. You can't miss it."

"How will I recognize him?"

He gave me a look you'd give a slow child. "He'll recognize you. You'll be the only one he doesn't know."

In spite of Janda's optimism, I suddenly felt I was marching in place. Janicki probably couldn't tell me anything, even if he wanted to.

"Stan," I said, "if Bartodziec didn't tell his wife about his financial affairs, he probably didn't tell his friends."

"That's not necessarily the way it works," he said. "Old World attitudes prevail here. The wife takes care of the house, the kids, the shopping. Finances are none of her business. For her own good, of course."

"Helen Bartodziec worked," I said.

He grinned. "Doesn't matter. This isn't exactly Betty Friedan country."

I hit the Kennedy heading for the Loop, troubled with the thought that false progress is worse than no progress at all. Failure seemed to be circling above me like vultures waiting for something to die. It wasn't only this case, but Stan's reminder of Judge Patrick A. Walsh. He was a no-class boor who never got the hang of scratching his nuts through his robes, which never kept him from trying. In the middle of a trial he'd stand up, drawing to him every eye in the courtroom. Lawyers would stop talking in mid-sentence to look up at him, and all Walsh was trying to do was get a better reach.

Everyone knew how he'd gotten on the bench, the mystery was how he'd ever made it through law school. Dumb as a mullet. He'd been fired by a string of firms for abject incompetence, then when no one would hire him he opened his own practice, which was hopelessly unsuccessful. After a couple of malpractice suits, he could no longer get insurance. But Walsh had one shining quality: He was a brilliant precinct captain, delivered the vote to his party as faithfully as a golden retriever fetches the morning paper. It was said that one year he delivered more votes in his precinct than there were voters. His party organization, nothing if not loyal, showed its gratitude. Walsh was still on the bench, and he'd cost me my law license.

It happened in the middle of the trial. My opponent was arguing a spurious motion. At the time, I didn't know he'd contributed heavily to the judge's re-election campaign. He was asking the judge to bar my client from testifying, claiming that my client had not turned over certain documents. It was a ridiculous ploy. The documents had no relevance to the case, and I told the judge that anyway the documents had been destroyed long before suit was filed.

"He's lying," my opponent said.

Just like that, he called me a liar. I kept my cool, said simply, "Your Honor, he's way out of line. Please admonish counsel."

Judge Walsh said, "Why don't you quit lying?"

Then my opponent said, "Yeah, just quit lying."

I took a breath. "Your honor, I've been called a liar by both of you. That is a very, very serious thing. Perhaps, because it came in the heat of the moment, you regret it. If you want to retract it, there will be no hard feelings."

Walsh gave an incredulous little huff. "Mr. Duncavan, you're seriously out of order," he said. But he didn't leave it at that. It was as though he wanted to drill a hole in me, fill it with insult. "You're out of order, and you're lying."

My opponent snickered like a donkey, and that's when I lost it. I grabbed his tie, pulling his face into the punch, and his knees gave way, and then the deputy bolted over, tried to grab my arm, and I decked him, too. Walsh was hustling down off the bench now, terror in his eyes, lifting his robe like a woman and crying in a falsetto, "Sheriff, my God, someone call the sheriff," and I caught him with a roundhouse punch that put him flat on the floor. When it was over, I felt really bad about the deputy.

I knew there was no defense, and I took my punishment. But the hardest thing was that absolutely no one seemed to understand; it was as though the notion of honor had become lost to the world. How odd that my father, never close, never a touchy-feely guy, would have understood, and I could imagine him throwing an arm over my shoulder, saying, "It's all right, son. You don't let a man

toy with your honor. You got to back up to the wall, but if
you can't back up no farther, you don't let a man insult
your honor."

Of course there was no hope of keeping my law license,
and I didn't even fight the disbarment proceedings,
knowing what the legal fees would have been, and that there
wasn't much chance anyway. Besides, keeping my license
would have meant showing remorse, and I had no remorse.
No one seemed to understand, though, that there are some
things you just don't let pass. Marty Richter, my old homicide partner, understood, but he still thought I was a damn
fool. Homicide detectives understand things other people
don't, though. They understand why people get killed when
everyone else is baffled; understand, for example, that when
a man is living in the world's underbelly, you never know
what he's got left, what might be the only thing he's
clinging to, and that when you try to take that away, he will
try to kill you. Sometimes it's his honor, sometimes it's
something only he knows about. That's why, in the streets
where decay hangs like garland in the air, death comes so
swiftly and so often. Hell, all I did was punch a judge.

One time Richter and I handled a homicide in front of a
theater. "You ain't gonna believe this one," the patrolman
said. "They're standing in line to get tickets, see, and this
guy takes a step back, accidentally steps on the guy's toes
behind him. The one behind him pulls a .32 auto, blows
him away. Emptied the fucking gun."

A few hours later, the shooter was sitting in the interrogation room, tears streaming down his cheeks, telling us he
didn't know why he did it. But I knew. He'd lost his job, his
wife had just left him, taken his kids, moved back to Missis-
sippi. He was being evicted from his apartment. And he had
the shiniest shoes I ever saw.

★ ★ ★ ★ ★

When I got to my office, I called Sylvia Westbrook, an acquaintance in the CTA's legal department. Hoping to cut some red tape, I told her I needed a favor, a look at the employment records of Robert Norton, Watson's former tenant. "Sylvia, I hate to ask, but I don't have time to go through all the red tape."

I could tell, when she took a long time to respond, that I'd put her on the spot. "Sorry, Mike, I can't. There's no way we can release that information."

"Tell you what. How about I give you a subpoena?"

"Well, of course, you can always subpoena the records. I thought you said you were in a hurry."

"I am. How about I hand-deliver a subpoena, then I'll take a look at the file right there?"

"Well—that sounds like a plan. I'll call you back in ten minutes."

"Sylvia, thanks. I really owe you one."

"Look, Mike, I can't promise. But you're just going to stand here and look at the file, right? You don't expect to take it with you?"

"Of course not. I'm looking for an address. If you want to look in the file yourself and give me the address, it could save us both a lot of—"

"Sorry, Mike, no way. I'll call you back, all right?"

Five minutes later, she called. "It's all set. Go to Human Resources, ask for Loretta Armstrong. Make sure you bring the subpoena." Before she hung up, she hesitated. "Mike," she said. "How are things going with you? You doing okay?"

"Better by the minute," I said, thanked her again, and said goodbye.

I rolled a blank subpoena into the typewriter, filled in

the blanks, walked it over to the court clerk's office, got it officially stamped, then headed for the CTA offices in the Merchandise Mart across the river. Loretta Armstrong, a pleasant, middle-aged black woman, greeted me at the counter, evidently waiting for me. "Mr. Duncavan?"

I nodded.

"Got the file right here," she said.

I handed her the subpoena, she handed over the file, then stood across the counter within arm's reach as I went through it, smiling pleasantly each time I raised my eyes.

Robert Norton was retired, but his last address was on Burling, near Division. I jotted down the address and his phone number, thanked Ms. Armstrong, and as I walked down the wide corridor, dialed Norton's number on my cell phone, hoping it was still a good one. It was; Norton answered. I told him I was working on a case for Moses Watson, hoping there'd been good will between them. "I'd like to stop by and talk to you, whenever it's convenient."

"Moses Watson's one of the best," he said. "Don't make 'em like Moses no mo'. I'll help any way I can, but you caught me on the way out. Can you come by tomorrow?"

I told him I'd be there at eleven. There are real benefits in having a well-liked client.

I drove home, ate dinner, fed Stapler, poured myself a Stoli on the rocks, and sat in my big easy chair in the living room, sipping and thinking. Suddenly I remembered the pieces of the note I'd recovered, still in the pocket of my sport coat. I retrieved them, spread them on the dining room table, sorted them like a jigsaw puzzle. There were only eight pieces, and when I put them together, it said:

Milk

Margarine

Shredded Wheat

Tampons
2 btl. Ginger Ale

That night I dreamed of her, the woman who'd torn up the note. We were in a courtroom, she was a prosecutor and I was the defendant, indicted for unspecified crimes of maleness. She fixed me with that smoldering look as I sat in the dock horrified, unrepresented, having been unable to find a lawyer who'd defend such unadulterated, testosterone-induced acts of loathsomeness. I scanned the faces of the jury, all either pissed-off women or dorky men. Then the phone woke me. I snatched it up, looking over at the numbers glowing on the clock: one-fourteen.

"Those people over there, right now," the voice said. It took several seconds to realize I was talking to Errol Flynn. "Came back in that ratty-ass station wagon, no muffler, mu-fuckuh woke me up. Somebody come in a Buick, too."

I thanked him, sat on the edge of the bed for several seconds, my brain still wooly with sleep, trying to decide what to do. Call the police? But there was no crime, and it was in a different district, and I had no standing as a complaining witness, anyway. I pulled on some clothes, slipped on the shoulder holster with the .357, pulled on a baggy tee shirt, grabbed the keys to Watson's building, and drove over there.

The streets were deserted at that hour, but I still had to wait for the long light at Armitage and Ashland, and after that I just kept an eye out for cops and drove through the red lights. It took me less than fifteen minutes, but as soon as I turned into Watson's block I could see that the station wagon was gone. I slowed, then spotted the Buick, parked facing the other way. As I neared, a woman stepped quickly from around the back of the car, opened the door, and got in. I pulled up next to her. She started the car, looking over at me, expressionless, dark-skinned, thin-faced, big, round eyes, shoulder-length, shiny hair. I signaled with my hand through the open window. "Just a minute," I said. Her window was closed. She dropped the car into gear, floored the accelerator, and squealed off down the street.

Facing the wrong way, I sped to the end of the block, keeping an eye on her in my rearview mirror. Her brake lights came on at the first intersection, she turned left. By the time I got turned around, followed to the intersection, her tail lights were nowhere in sight. I drove that street for several blocks, looking down each passing street both ways for tail lights. Nothing.

I drove back to the building and parked in front, and as I got out a figure detached itself from the shadow across the street, and Errol Flynn drifted over. I opened my wallet, which contained one twenty and one single. I handed him the twenty.

"Thank you," he said, slipping it into his pants pocket. "The station wagon pulled away about two minutes before you got here. Still want me to call you if I see anything?"

"Yeah. Thanks," I said, thinking I'd better get an advance from Artemus Shumway. After saying goodnight, I let myself into Moses' building, flipped on my flashlight and went straight to the basement. The wooden chest was gone.

I drove home wondering if I should be chasing this down, whether it was drawing my attention away from the murder. Security for the building was Danny McGarry's worry, not mine. Still, I didn't have any solid leads. And I still felt there was some connection.

Chapter Nine

Before I left home the following morning, I called my old homicide partner, Marty Richter, now a watch commander at the Deering station. I needed a fresh, objective look at this picture. Marty and I went back a distance, beyond the police department. We were classmates at St. Rita High School on the south side; I was godfather to his daughter, Angela, now a social worker in Minneapolis. We kept in touch, met for dinner irregularly. Our minds ran in similar channels. That could have been a disadvantage, but I trusted Marty's street smarts more than any other copper's.

The patrolman at the desk said Lieutenant Richter was conducting roll call and took a message. Marty called me back ten minutes later. "I thought you died," he said.

"No you didn't. You read the obituaries every morning before you take a dump. Listen, I'd like to run something by you, a case I'm working on."

"Sure, what's up?"

"It's a kind of a long story," I said. I thought it would be better to explain it face-to-face, but the running of the clock loomed like an approaching locomotive. "You got a minute?"

"Yeah, I'm not going anywhere."

I told him about Bartodziec's murder, the money left in his wallet, and about Watson, the kind of guy he was, that he could lose his building. Then I said, "Look, this is a little embarrassing, so I'd appreciate it if you don't laugh, but—"

88

I told him about finding the gorilla skeleton, about reporting it to the police as a homicide, and about the phone call to the detectives the next day. When I finished, there was only silence. "Hello?" I said.

Laughter gushed like a dam bursting. I thought he would never stop. When finally it fell to a trickle, I said, "You finished?"

"Yeah, sorry," he said, and hooted a couple more times. "Look," he said, "Charley Dykes is the commander at Area One Violent Crimes now. Why don't you talk to him, find out what he knows?"

"Charley Dykes hates my guts," I said.

"You're wrong about that. Last time I saw him, he asked me how you were getting along. He seemed very concerned, Mike, very sincere. Besides, he's a good guy. Tell you what, why don't I call him? I'll meet you at Bennigan's at five-thirty, let you know what I find out."

I drove to the office thinking about Charley Dykes. He was a sergeant back then. Charley had a special hatred for newspaper reporters, but I didn't know that. One time I dropped by a homicide scene. Charley was there, and so was a guy from my night law school class, then a reporter for the *Chicago Daily News*. I talked to the guy for a few minutes, and introduced him to Charley. Then I left, assuming Charley knew he was a reporter, since they were both there before me. But Charley for some reason assumed the guy was a policeman, probably because he thought no real policemen would ever introduce a lowlife reporter to anybody, especially to his sergeant. So Charley embarrassed himself, told the reporter a lot of stuff he would never have told him otherwise.

I found out about it at roll call the next morning, Charley Dykes sitting behind his desk, the day crew leaning against the walls and file cabinets around the squad room. Livid, punching out his words, Sergeant Dykes recounted the incident, the first I'd heard about it. Had I been Dykes, I'd have kept my mouth shut. It didn't make him look like the brightest bulb on the tree. But when he finished, he looked straight at me and said, "If I ever see you even talking to a reporter again, Duncavan, I'll punch your lights out, right there."

It was a public humiliation, and a white flash of anger ignited in my brain. I took three strides, put my hands on his desk and my nose close to his. "You don't have the balls, Dykes. Want to show me what you got right now?"

Then Richter snatched my arm, yanked me out the door. "Hey, Sarge," he called over his shoulder, "we're gonna hit the street now, okay?"

Dykes may have been way off base, but I could have been fired. It wasn't just insubordination—the department took an even dimmer view of armed men physically challenging one another. That was conduct set off by a bright yellow line. But Dykes never said another word about it, ever. And no one else ever brought it up, at least not to me. It was as if the whole thing never happened—except from that day on, Dykes' eyes would ricochet off mine every time we met.

It was a reminder, though, of the downside of that cozy fraternity. Membership required that you talk the talk and walk the walk, always. The walk and the talk came naturally enough; but I couldn't always think the think, and that too could brand you as an outsider. And what kind of pinko liberal shitbird would befriend a newspaper reporter?

At eleven I was ringing the doorbell of Robert Norton, the retired CTA driver who'd lived across the hall from Moses Watson. Now he was living on the first floor of a two-flat building with his daughter and her kids, and he invited me into the living room, windows open to the street, kids running in and out. Heavy-set and sweating, shaved head shiny as a bowling ball, Norton sat with his arms on knees, bent over a huge belly.

"I'm afraid I can't be of much help," he said. "Much as I like Moses, I wasn't there when the guy got shot."

"Do you remember the lock on the front door being broken?"

"Coulda been. Don't remember that, though."

"Do you know anything about drug dealing in a vacant apartment?"

"There wasn't no vacant apartments, I can tell you that much. It was a real nice building, people always wanting to move in. I'd still be there, hadn't been for the fire."

"You're sure? What about drug dealing?"

"Neighborhood's fulla dope. Could be somebody in the building was dealing. I mind my business, never had nothing to do with that shit. I doubt it, though. Like I say, it was a nice building. For sure, there weren't no vacant apartments."

"Mr. Norton, will you testify to that in court?"

"Yeah. Well, maybe they was vacant for a few weeks, something like that. If someone moved out in the middle of the month, say. But that would be all. Mostly, people just stayed."

"What about Calvin Clark, who lived on the second floor?"

"Yeah, I knew Calvin. He died, you know. What about Calvin?"

"After he died, was his apartment vacant?"

He thought a minute. "I can't recollect when it was he died, exactly, whether it was before or after the guy got shot."

"But was his apartment vacant after he died?"

He ran a hand over the top of his head. "Maybe for a little while, but not for long."

"I'd like to talk to some of the other tenants. You ever see any of them?"

"No. Well, Fannie Walker, I see Fannie now and then. She was livin' over there on Orchard and Willow, right on the northeast corner. I think she still livin' there."

It had been Fannie who'd heard the shots, called the police. I jotted that down in my note book, then took a card from my wallet. "One more thing. Do you know anything about voodoo in the neighborhood?"

"Voodoo?" He laughed. "Sure don't."

"Mr. Norton," I said, handing him my card, "if you ever see any of the other tenants, or maybe hear something about the shooting, please call me, okay?"

I drove directly to Willow and Burling, buoyed with the feeling, perhaps delusional, that I was getting somewhere. Norton's testimony, that the building had no vacant apartments, was equivocal and probably of no help, especially since he said Calvin Clark's apartment may have been vacant for awhile. That was the apartment where the drug deals were supposed to be going down. His testimony that Moses kept a nice, clean building would definitely help, if Artemus could get it past Lagatee's objection. I knew Hollis Lagatee. He'd argue that testimony about the cleanliness of the building was prejudicial to his client, since it had no bearing on the real issues, which were: whether the locks were broken, whether crimes were committed in the hallways, whether drugs were being dealt out of a vacant apartment. And technically, he'd be right.

But I also knew that Shavonne Sykes, whatever her motive was, couldn't wait to dump all over Moses; that was clear from the tone of her affidavit. And knowing Lagatee, he would not be inclined to hold her back. She'd probably call the building a pigsty and, as lawyers are fond of saying, "open the door" for Norton's rebuttal testimony.

And I'd found Fannie Walker, or was close. I parked in front of the building, a six-flat with a center entrance, and found I was in luck: the name "Walker" was hand-printed on a strip of masking tape on one mailbox. I rang the bell and waited, then rang it again. No answer. Sometimes luck goes just so far.

When I arrived at Bennigan's at five, Marty Richter was already at the bar sipping a martini, easy to spot with that rich crop of silver hair. In the old days Marty could run faster than me, but now, noting the development of his girth, I doubted he was inclined to run at all. We had one drink at the bar, ordered another, carried it to a table for dinner.

"I talked to Charley Dykes today," Marty said, opening the menu. "You've got it all wrong about Dykes. He said you should have called him. He asked again how you're doing. The guys in his unit, they were just having a little fun with you. Mike . . ." he said, and his voice trailed off. He smiled to himself, shook his head and took a sip of his drink.

"What?"

"Nothing."

"No, what were you going to say?"

He put his drink down. "There're times when you can't seem to take a joke. I mean, sometimes you'd be a lot better off if you'd just lighten up. They were ribbing you a little, for Christ sake."

"When I saw the skeleton, I reported it. I never went up close. I wasn't going to go pawing around, fucking up a crime scene."

"Hey, don't get all defensive, okay?" He laughed.

93

"Actually you did the Property Crimes guys a big favor, you know that? The gorilla skeleton was taken in a burglary from the Adventurer's Club of Chicago. They took all kinds of shit out of there, and it was all piled down there with the skeleton. Hyena bones, walrus tusks, all kinds of stuff—it was all there with the gorilla. The Adventurer's never expected they'd get that stuff back. In Property Crimes, you're a fucking hero. Probably at the Adventurer's Club, too. Really, those were all mementos, a lot of them very old. Irreplaceable."

"From a distance it looked human, Marty. It was dressed in a suit."

"Yeah, I know. Some of that old-fashioned, Adventurer's Club humor, I guess. They kept it in a glass case at the club. It had been there a long time, came from a zoo way back in the thirties. You missed the whale penis, buddy."

"What?"

He nodded. "That's right, about five feet long, Charley said, laying right there under the gorilla skeleton. 'Course they didn't know what it was at first. The club had it hanging up over the bar."

The waitress came over. We ordered dinner, and she brought us another round of drinks. "What do you think, Marty?" I said. "You got any ideas? I'm fresh out."

He scanned the table for a spoon and, finding none, stirred his martini with his fingertip. "I think whatever's going on in that basement is a distraction." He sucked his finger. "I think you should forget about it."

"I know. But I just got this hunch, there's a connection somehow."

"How's that?"

I lifted my shoulders. "A hunch."

"Look, maybe you're right, maybe there's a connection,

but that don't make it a great lead. It's a fucking red herring. What you need is an eyeball, or at least somebody who knows why the Polack got it."

"I know."

"I know you know. Forget about all that drum-banging, weird shit in the basement. Anyway, that's my advice. But at the same time, you better get the building secured. I'll guarantee you, any illegal activity in that building, the city'll turn it into a pile of bricks in the blink of an eye."

"Right, which brings up another point. I'm wondering if what's going on is even illegal. I mean, there's no crime in banging drums and chanting, is there? So suppose they're killing animals in some ritual. Is that illegal?"

He shrugged, snapped open a Zippo with a gold Marine Corps emblem, lit a cigarette. "You got me on that one." He turned a little sideways, blew out a stream of smoke. "You're the lawyer," he said. Then he looked away, red-faced.

"Marty, it's okay," I said.

"Mike, I don't know what you care if it's legal or illegal, you asked my advice. You've got to concentrate on what went down the night of the murder."

"I know. I care because if it's illegal, the city's got a reason to tear down the building. But with all the tenants gone, finding anything out about the shooting looks pretty dismal. Listen, do this for me, will you? See what you can find out about voodoo in the neighborhood."

"I'll ask around, pardner. And you concentrate on finding an eyeball."

Thursday, August 10

The following evening when I drove over to meet Florian

Janicki, Milwaukee Avenue was clogged with traffic, sidewalks swarming with pedestrians, and I couldn't find a parking space near Wanda's. I finally found one on a side street about three blocks away, and as I walked back in the lowering sun, the air felt like warm insulation clinging to your skin. Lined on both sides with two-story bungalows, aluminum-sided, high front stoops, the street hummed with activity: people everywhere, women sitting on porches, men in undershirts talking across fences, kids running on the small, neat squares of lawn. Polish was the only language I heard. At one corner there had been a minor traffic accident, the two cars pulled over at the curb, a policeman taking statements from the drivers. One driver was interpreting for the other.

The door of Wanda's stood open, the interior dark and cool, tables standing in shadow along the walls, the rectangular bar an island of light. Twenty minutes early, I pulled out a stool at the bar, eyes adjusting gradually to the darkness. The bartender came over, a woman I guessed was Wanda, plump in a black dress, dyed black hair, sixty-five trying to look thirty-nine. She smiled cordially, asked in that precise Polish accent what I'd like. I ordered a double Stoli on the rocks, thinking how you can tell a foreigner by the way they speak English better than we do. No dropped consonants, no contractions, no slurred speech.

The track lighting above the bar felt like a spotlight, and I sensed eyes scrutinizing me from the shadows. I considered moving to a table but decided against it, and sipped my Stoli, pretending to mind my own business, now and then stealing a look at the faces around the bar. Weariness seemed the condition of the hour: faces sagging, heads sunk into shoulders.

After awhile I picked up on an argument in progress at a

table to my left: low, angry voices, a man and woman. She wore a red dress, her blonde, wavy hair highlighted in the track lighting, her shadowed face turned away from the man. He had a pinched face, razor-cut hair, black with gray streaks swept back, dressed in a tan summer suit. He leaned over his cuff links, his face close to hers, voice low and supplicant, a tone you might use to tell a cop the light actually was green. It sounded like English, but I wasn't sure. I tried not to stare, but they were pretty absorbed in each other anyway. At one point, his face close to hers, he stopped talking. She wasn't looking at him. Then she shook her head emphatically, hissed something, and snatched up her purse. I thought she was walking out, but she breezed past me toward the ladies' room, and I caught a whiff of her perfume. It was captivating. She was well put together, long-legged, hair the color of honey, haughty carriage, shoulders back, chin high. The guy sat there staring at the table top for a minute, then swept up the change, folded the bills into his pocket, and walked out.

When she caught sight of the empty table on her way back she seemed disconcerted. She paused for a few seconds standing next to me, her perfume toying with my heart, then she went to the table and sat down alone and dug into her purse for a pack of cigarettes. She lit one and leaned back, jaw set, staring at something far away. She had high cheekbones and a classically beautiful face.

I ordered another Stoli, tempted to ask the bartender to get one for the lady too, but I resisted, reminding myself that I was here on business. I finished that one and the bartender was bringing me a third when someone climbed onto the stool next to me. "Mr. Mike," he said. He was a fireplug of a guy, five-six, mid-forties, round, pudgy face, thick, greasy brown hair combed straight back, a little long around the ears and collar. "Florian Janicki," he said. His hand closed on mine like pliers. I thanked him for coming, asked what he'd like.

"She's getting it," he said, nodding toward the bartender. Wanda was drawing a Miller Genuine Draft. She brought it over, set it in front of Florian with a shot glass, then filled the shot glass with whiskey. He said something to her in Polish without looking at her. She smiled, moved away.

"Look, I tell you right now, I don't like this," he said. "Tadeusz was my friend. Stanley Janda, him I owe my life to. He tells me you are his friend and I should tell you the truth. So I tell you the truth, that's it." He knocked back the shot, took a long pull on his beer. "That's it, so ask me."

"How well did you know Tadeusz?"

He pulled a wrist across his mouth and looked at me like I was some kind of clown. "How well I know him? He live here, I live here," he said, bouncing a fat finger twice on the bar. "I get him job in machine shop, together every day we go to work, Milwaukee Avenue bus to el to machine shop. Walking, every day."

"Florian, do you have any idea what Tadeusz was doing in that building that night?"

He shook his head, took another pull on his beer, wiped his mouth with the back of his hand again, and sat staring at himself in the mirror. He wasn't going to make this easy.

"Did Tadeusz ever use drugs?"

Before I finished the sentence he was shaking his head vigorously. "He never, never use drugs. This I know."

"Okay," I said. "But what about . . . dealing?"

"You mean like, sell drugs?"

I shrugged, turning my hands up, and again he shook his

head vigorously. "No, no, not Tadeusz. If you know him you don't even ask such a question. Tadeusz? Hah!"

"Okay. Did he have any special interests? Hobbies?"

"Hobbies?" His head jerked back in a laugh. "Hobbies? Yes, his family, his jobs. Two jobs he worked, how the fuck he will have hobbies?" He drained his beer and caught Wanda's eye. She got off her stool, came over, and took his glass.

He was growing hostile, and I thought Janda's name, the guy he owed, might bring him gentler thoughts of me. "Florian, like Mr. Janda told you, I'm not trying to hurt anyone. I'm just after the truth." I hesitated. "You know, Janda and me, we go way back. Way, way, back. Guy's a prince, isn't he?"

It was shameless, but I saw his shoulders relax a little. "Don't come no better than Mr. Janda." Wanda glided over carrying a draft beer in one hand and a whiskey bottle in the other, set the beer down in front of Florian and poured him another shot. He looked at me and bobbed his head once. "Sure. I'm sorry. What can I tell you?"

"Hey, the question about hobbies—stupid, you're right. But he had dreams, didn't he? What were his dreams?"

"His dreams? What we all dream was his dreams. What everyone comes to this country for. Better life for family. That was his dream." He looked out the open door, into the twilight falling across Milwaukee Avenue. A CTA bus ambled past. "He was good man, Tadeusz. He was prince, too." I let him remember. "But too much pride he had. His pride, his honor, make always too much for fighting. Very tough guy, Tadeusz. You fuck with Tadeusz, you got big troubles."

"Did he get in trouble with the police?"

"Only with fighting. He fighting, police come, he fight

99

police, too. Very tough, that Tadeusz. But he was good man, good father. You know, all times he worry, worry. His savings not getting bigger. Very little interest, the bank pays. Almost nothing."

"Did he have much money saved?"

He laughed. "You think he tell me this? Oh, brother, you don't know these Polacks. A Polack, he don't tell you nothing about his money."

I ordered another Stoli, deciding not to press him. As Wanda poured my drink, I was having trouble keeping my eyes off the blonde at the table, her crossed leg exposing a length of creamy thigh, the light chiseling her high cheeks, deepening the sweet mystery of her cleavage. I sipped my Stoli, and Florian tossed back his shot, gulped at his beer, wiped his mouth again, then seemed to remember something.

"This I know. Tadeusz wanted to buy building. Looking for building to buy, but he did not have money enough. Then some guy talking to him about—" he thought a moment. "I cannot think of the word. For putting money with other people together?"

"Partnership?"

"Bingo, partnership."

"Who was the guy?"

"I don't know him. It was long time ago." He looked at his watch. "Sorry, I have to go." He waved to Wanda and slid off the stool, pulling out his wallet.

"No, it's on me." I looked at Wanda, tapped a twenty on the bar. Florian smiled, shook his head, pulled some bills from his wallet.

"No, really, I got it," I said, grabbing the twenty, handing it to Wanda.

"No!" It was almost a shout. "*I* pay," he said. "I am not

informer." He was no longer smiling. He counted out eight singles onto the bar and said good night.

I ordered another Stoli, hoping I hadn't offended him. Tenuous as it was, he was the only thread leading to the mind of Tadeusz Bartodziec. I finished the Stoli and ordered another, noticing through the open door that daylight had fled. The Stoli was working on me; I was feeling expansive. The Lady in Red was staring off somewhere, chin on sculpted fingertip. I couldn't take my eyes off her. She finished her drink, then leaning forward, folded her arms on the table, her wares coming into better view. I signaled for Wanda, asked her to see if the lady would like another drink. Wanda looked at me levelly for a second. It was a message that, probably because of the booze, I disregarded. She went over and whispered something to the lady. The lady shook her head as though she'd swallowed something bitter. She did not look at me; at least I was spared that. I went to the john and when I came back, she was gone. Win some, lose some, I thought. Still feeling pretty charming, I gave Wanda a champion's kind of smile and asked what I owed her. She did not smile back. Win some, lose some, a voice in my head repeated; it sounded like the Stoli.

I paid, headed out into the summer night, and stood a moment trying to recall where I'd left my car. I started walking south, hoping I'd recognize the right side street, and heard muffled, angry voices coming from somewhere. I looked around, didn't see anybody, and continued walking, and I heard it again, with a grunt this time, and a woman's distraught voice, coming from around the corner. I trotted the few feet to the end of the block and caught sight of them, lit by the street lamp at the mouth of the alley, the Lady in Red and a male figure pulling at her purse. She was cursing him, hanging on. He grabbed hold of her arm, started to twist it, and she started screaming, "No! No!" I sprinted the distance, starting the right hook before I got there, then with the full force of my body drove my fist into the side of his head. He seemed to lift a little, then sprawled on the pavement, a short wiry guy. For a second, he didn't move, didn't even make a sound.

I turned to her, saw that the sleeve of her dress was torn. And then she looked at me with panic in her eyes, and it confused me for a second and too late I saw she was looking past me and suddenly someone with biceps like fieldstones had his arms wrapped around me, pinning my own arms. His breath quivered against my ear.

He shouted something in Spanish, and the one lying on the sidewalk began to raise himself. Now I fought to pull away from him and we staggered in a small circle as the other one got to his feet in stages. It was useless to struggle, and I stopped. The one getting up shook his head hard, then face lowered, he came to me, taking his time. The Lady in Red was at his side then, pleading with him, but he ignored her, slipping a hand into his front pocket. I felt my bowels pucker, knowing what was coming, knowing my only hope was to relax. He had the blade in his hand, then, a flash of steel in the light from the street lamp. Taco breath behind me barked something again, and the other lifted the knife to my face. No longer struggling, I felt the arms around me relax just a little. The Lady in Red was poking her purse into the face of the one with the knife, screaming at him to take it. Confused, he looked at it a moment, then he grabbed for it, but she snatched it away, threw it out into the street.

His eyes darted to the purse, to his partner, to the purse again, and then he dashed into the street to get it, and the guy behind me screamed something at him in Spanish and I bent, reached between my legs, and snatched his ankles, jerked them up off the ground, and when I heard the crack of his head on the pavement I pivoted on one foot and drove the other foot into his face.

"Look out!" the lady screamed.

Without looking I dodged, felt the other one carom off my shoulder, his foot tangled in mine, and he was falling, grabbing at my shirt, and I kicked him once and he went down but was quickly regaining his feet, and I caught him with a left jab to the side of the head, followed with a long, solid roundhouse to the middle of his face and felt the bones of his nose splinter, and followed with two quick left jabs. He went down again, let out a deep grunt and rolled over. This time he looked like he was down to stay.

I stepped on his wrist, bent to take the knife from him, but it was gone.

"Lady, just get the hell out of here," I shouted, not knowing whether they were down for the count, or whether they had any more pals around, but then the building at the corner started pulsating in a blue and red light, and a squad car came around the corner, followed seconds later by another. They were out of the car and had the two in handcuffs in seconds.

"You're bleeding!" said the Lady in Red. I felt it then, a burning pain, and craned around to see blood oozing through a slice in my shirt near the top of my shoulder. The little prick really did cut me. I looked at him lying on the ground in handcuffs, and an old fire leapt from my belly, igniting my brain. This little fucker *cut* me!

"You, little, *cocksucker!*" I lunged for him, a dagger of pain ripping though my ankle. I nearly stumbled, and one of the cops stepped in front of me. I hobbled around him. *"This scumbucket cut me!"* I yelled and reached down for the front of the guy's shirt, but the cop was in front of me again, pushing me back, and I slammed both hands into the cop's chest and shoved him hard, sent him reeling, and in an instant his partner was behind me, and the two of them had my arms pinned behind my back. They handcuffed me.

A squadron came, drove off with the two gang-bangers. I in my handcuffs rode to the station in the back of the squad car, ankle throbbing, back sticky with blood. I was unsure of my own status, though from the strictures upon my wrists, it was fair to say I was not a free man. I knew I was on thin ice, having assaulted a police officer. If I were them, I'd have locked up my ruddy Irish ass and thrown away the key. But the Lady in Red sitting beside me was pleading my case, telling them what a hero I was. The way they looked her over, I knew I couldn't have had a better lawyer.

They wanted to take me to the hospital, but I refused, and when we got to the station they took the cuffs off, told me I could go as soon as the paperwork was done. I apologized; the one I had shoved punched my good shoulder hard, and laughed. They offered one last time to take me to the emergency room. Actually my ankle, throbbing like an abscessed tooth, hurt worse than my shoulder, but in any case going to the emergency room would mean saying goodbye to the Lady in Red. I was trying to read the script for the rest of the evening. The Lady in Red could not let this poor devil go home to tend his wound all alone.

Her name, she told the cops, was Marie Galkowska. She signed complaints, and the cops said they'd drive us wherever we wanted to go. When we pulled up in front of Marie's house, one of those two-story bungalows with the high front stairs, I got out with her. She did not object.

"Thank you," she said as we stood on the sidewalk in front of her house.

"Don't mention it," I said, that high front stoop to her apartment seeming like a stairway to heaven. Finally I said, "I'd still like to buy you a drink."

"You should really go to the hospital," she said.

I shook my head, smiling oh-so-stoically.

"Will you come up and let me have a look at it?"

I would have danced up those stairs like Fred Astaire, even though my ankle was killing me.

Her apartment was neat, an abundance of leather and chrome, the painting over the couch an abstraction of frenzied color. She led me to the bathroom, told me to take off my shirt. I obeyed. The back of it was soaked in brown blood. She had me sit on the toilet seat, my back to her, while she found some bandages and gauze and iodine in the medicine cabinet. When she looked at my shoulder, her hand shot to her mouth. "Oh!" she said, and faced me. "You should have that sewed."

"Sewed?" the stoical one asked with amusement.

"Sewed, yes. Look." She took hold of my bare arms, the warmth of her hands stirring my groin, and stood me up, turned me so I could see over my shoulder in the mirror. When I saw it, a gash about four inches long, gaping like an idiot's smile, I nearly puked.

I shrugged with my good shoulder, hoping not to up-chuck, hoping she did not notice the color drain from my face. She spilled iodine on a wad of cotton, and when she swabbed it on I yelled: "Fuck!" I felt like I'd been branded.

"You asked for it," she said. She scissored some butter-flies out of surgical tape, brought the edges of the wound together, and closed it with the bandage. "You must work out," she said, smoothing the tape across my right deltoid.

"I try," I said modestly.

"Then where does this come from?" She reached round,

patted my gut, then ran her hands along my sides. "I think these are called, what, lover's handles?" Then her hand brushed the rough circular scar of the exit wound, and her eyes lifted to mine in the mirror. I was grateful she did not ask about it. Instead she picked up the bloody shirt from the floor and said, "You can't wear this. Come with me."

I followed her through the kitchen, where she dropped the shirt in the garbage, to a back bedroom. She slid open the closet door, the compressed contents looking about to reach critical mass. Dresses, skirts, blouses, slacks on hangars, shoes in heaps on the floor. She reached to the very end, seized several shirts, snatched them out, tossed them on a chair—men's shirts. She lifted one to my chest, leaned back, appraising. "This will fit you," she said. "You can keep it. You can keep all of them."

Before I could say anything she moved her face close to mine, fixing me with her eyes, softening now. "Thank you again," she said, and kissed me, her lips lingering, then kissed me again and again, urgently, one hand caressing the back of my head. Then her hands descended, deft fingers opening my fly. She slipped to her knees, took me in hand. This was not what I had in mind. I took her arms, gently tugged. She stood, led me to the bed. "Lie down," she said.

I did, and she knelt next to the bed, took me in hand again, careful with her sculpted nails, shiny red and studded with tiny rhinestones. Like the woman who copied Bartodziec's letters, I thought. I could never look at those again without becoming aroused. Again I reached to pull her to me, but she shook her head. "No," she said, pushing me back, giving me a sly smile. "You've had a hard night," she said. "I'll help you relax." And with the slow, wet warmth of her mouth, she did.

When it was over, she asked if I'd like coffee. I asked if

she might have some vodka instead. She put on a pot of coffee for herself, set a bottle of vodka and a glass of ice in front of me. I glanced at my watch. It was late, she probably had to be up for work early, but I filled the glass to the brim anyway. There was a lot of ice. She looked over as I poured, then looked me in the eye. "Would you like a bigger glass?" she said.

I shook my head. "Listen, you probably have to get up for work in the morning. I'll just have a quick one and get going."

"It's okay, relax. I'm having a cup of coffee." She brought her cup to the table, sat down. "Tomorrow I think maybe I'll quit my job anyway. Maybe I don't even go in."

"What do you do?"

She poured milk in her coffee. "I work for an insurance agency, on Milwaukee Avenue. I work for a skunk."

"I see. You got another job all lined up?"

"No, but in two weeks I take my broker's license test. It will be easier, then. I'll find another job. So, what do you do? I'll bet you're a cop, right?"

"Not exactly." Odd that I still had not learned how to handle this question. "Private investigator. Used to be a lawyer, but I don't practice anymore. Before that, I was a cop."

She looked at me sideways, one eyebrow lifting a little, wondering whether to believe me. I changed the subject. "Look, I'm not one who should give other people employment advice, but don't you think you should find another job before you quit?"

She raised her eyes to mine over her cup, then put it down, keeping her eyes on me. "I am a fool, you see. I fell in love with my boss. He's married to a frigid woman, a shrew, but he has two children and he wants to wait until they can deal with it better. 'Wait,' he tells me, 'wait.' For years. 'As soon as they are a little older.' Then, 'as soon as they finish high school.' I wait for him. You know what? His youngest child graduated from high school in June!"

She punched out "June" as if it had contained all the folly of the entire year. I didn't say anything.

"Know what he told me tonight?"

I turned my palms up. "Wait 'til they finish college?"

She fought back a smile, then her eyes dampened and she looked away, composed herself, turned back to me. "He says he cannot leave now because his wife is pregnant. Can you believe it? This, this *shit* telling me that?" Her voice cracked. "For years, I am waiting for him."

I took a slug of vodka, trying to look sympathetic.

"For years, he is telling me he never sleeps with his wife, only with me. They have separate bedrooms, he is always telling me. And you know what? He is very jealous of me, too, if I even look at another man. This skunk. And you know what else? I never look at another man. Ever. I am very faithful to him. For years." Her voice cracked again, and a tear skipped down her cheek. She brushed it away with her wrist.

"Did he explain, um, how she got pregnant?"

"Sure. It was only one time, he said. Only one time for many years. After a party both of them were drunk, she pulling him into bed. He was so drunk, he didn't know what was happening. What kind of a fool does he think I am?"

I didn't think she wanted me to answer. I shook my head sensitively.

"Tonight, with you," she said, and stopped. "I am not a loose woman. Please believe me, I am not. I just . . ." She folded her hands on the table, stared at her thumbs. "Please forgive me. I think I just wanted to punish him."

"I feel so used!" I said. I patted her hand. "But if it'll make you feel better, would you like to use me again?"

She laughed then, blinking back tears, put the heel of her hand to her eye and got up. "It's late," she said.

At her front door, I said, "I'm not leaving without your phone number."

She poked around on a shelf near the telephone, found a note pad, scribbled two numbers, tore off the sheet, and handed it to me. "It's okay to call me at the office. I hope you do."

We stood there a moment. She stroked my cheek, her smile soft and vulnerable, deepening her hold on me. I took her thumb, kissed her fingers, and saw then that she had a scar too, a narrow cord of light-colored flesh across her wrist. I kissed that, too. She drew her hand away.

"Again. Thank you," she said. I gave her one last, lingering kiss.

After she closed the door behind me I hobbled down the stairs one at a time, heel first, foot rigid, but even with the throbbing in my ankle and the gnawing pain in my shoulder, I wanted to dance a jig. Really, I'm not a tough guy. I do not enjoy pain. But throughout my life, pain has followed me without relent, pursued me into every refuge. It began when I started boxing. My old man started me early, believing, perhaps rightly, that I was turning into a wuss.

Supposedly, when he was a small child, E. M. Forster said to his father, "I'd rather be a coward than brave, because people hurt you when you're brave." Bully for Forster. But I had a very different kind of father, to whom there was nothing in the world more pathetic than a crybaby. Every Saturday morning he piled the three of us into the black Ford—my older brother, my older cousin, and me—drove us down to the Catholic Youth Organization gym. It had not been a matter of choice. The other two had been going for some time—I was inducted into the weekly ritual following my ninth birthday. The CYO was located on south Michigan Avenue, in a poor, black neighborhood. All the better, according to Dad, since the shine kids were naturally tougher, and that would make me tougher, too.

I hated boxing, hated going down there every Saturday, but most of all, hated getting the shit punched out of me. I got through it, though. A simple matter of survival. I didn't care about winning, I only cared about not getting hurt. But after awhile I turned into a tolerable fighter, developing what the coaches called my "style." To my mind, that meant staying the hell out of my opponent's reach until I saw an opening, then going in with a fury brought on by the hope of deliverance. Fear was my motivator. It was the same fear that got me started power lifting, at age eleven, hoping for arms that would grow strong enough to save me. I was still too slow to be really good, but I held my own at the Golden Gloves for a few seasons, and in the end I guess I did learn something: you can actually tolerate a lot of pain if you have to. Better if you don't have to.

We had seen each other's scars, Marie and I, but we did not, thank God, talk about them. Scars, physical and other-wise, are the cruelest of life's milestones. Mine did not come from boxing. They commemorated twin passions: lust and anger. As the nuns in grade school used to note on my report card, my lack of self-control. When Marie, standing in her bathroom, found that milestone on my flank, I was grateful she didn't ask where it came from, almost as grateful as I was that night, that the bullet wasn't a couple of inches over. It only passed through—God, was it some cosmic joke?—my left lover's handle. No need for a colostomy, no drains, none of that nasty stuff. Still, it is a stigma, a commemoration to the folly of my lust. You could say, with not much poetic license, that I shot myself with my own dick. Longer and sharper, I could have just drilled myself and eliminated the middleman. That bullet arrived only a millisecond before the one through my ankle. That was a bad wound. I nearly lost the foot. If it had happened in reverse order—if the shot to the ankle had come first—things would have turned out differently. Maybe I'd have gotten no shots off, and maybe I'd be dead, and maybe another life would have been spared. Two lives, if you count the wreckage of the one left behind.

Chapter Ten

Friday, August 11

In my office the following morning, I resisted the temptation to phone Marie. There was an answering machine message from Sandie Sommers, Artemus Shumway's secretary. The hearing on Artemus' motion for summary judgment was set for two p.m. Artemus would like very much for me to be there, if I could make it.

I called Moses, told him that Bartodziec may have been looking for an apartment building to buy, around the time he was killed. "I know it's not much to go on, but were you thinking of selling the building, or maybe looking for a partner?"

"No, I sure wasn't."

"You're sure?"

"Course I'm sure. Might have been a good idea, but it never even crossed my mind."

So Bartodziec wanted to buy a building, and he was shot to death in a building that wasn't for sale. Not exactly what you'd call an investigative breakthrough.

I walked over to the courthouse to meet Artemus, not sure why he wanted me there. He probably thought keeping me involved would keep me motivated. He was paying me by the hour, why argue? Besides, he was the cagiest lawyer I knew.

I first came to know Artemus not through the law, but through fly fishing. We belonged to the same chapter of Trout Unlimited, though before I met him, I had already heard several of the Artemus Shumway legends, spun off in the wake of his career, tales of some ingenious, bold stroke which, at the last moment, snatched a case from defeat. Later, Artemus and I came to spend a lot of delightful hours together, knee-deep in trout streams, and once after a day's fishing, as we dried our socks in front of a popping oak fire, both of us grown mellow on bonded bourbon, I asked him directly about the authenticity of these tales. He asked me to be more specific. As I related them one by one, he would simply shake his head and demur, but he could not hide the dance of delight in his eyes.

If these stories were true, you'd think someone would have cried foul, skirting as they did the edges of fair play— yet I have never heard an ill word spoken of Artemus Shumway. Maybe it's because of his gift for bullshit— Artemus could charm the rake off a Las Vegas croupier. Once I watched him play upon his seductive pipes before the Seventh Circuit Court of Appeals, the black-robed justices looming up there like ravens watching a funeral, stony-faced at first, then softening, nodding, and finally smiling at Artemus, and when he remarked as how his opponent was so preeminent a lawyer that Artemus felt humbled, *privileged* even, to be in the same courtroom, the other lawyer was grinning, too. When you understand that about him, you can understand the strange paradox of Shumway, Goldman & Fortuna—why a firm that bills those kinds of fees still does insurance defense work, which commands the lowest hourly rate in the profession.

Twenty-five years ago, Artemus was head of the insurance defense department for Sullivan & Peters, a big silk-stocking firm with about ninety lawyers. The hourly rates charged by other departments in the firm, patent law or anti-trust, say, had grown to more than twice the fees charged to the insurance industry. There were a limited number of insurance companies, all big enough to practice "economies of scale" when it came to hiring lawyers. One day the partners voted to quit the insurance defense business altogether, and when they did, Artemus was invited to leave. He did, taking the insurance defense business with their blessing, along with Goldman, a young corporate tax guru, and Fortuna, already of anti-trust fame—distinctly without their blessing. Goldman and Fortuna saw something in Shumway their former partners had overlooked, something Artemus knew even better than tort law: how to make rain. The new firm recruited talented lawyers in other areas, opened new departments. Many of the lawyers, along with much of the business, drifted over from Sullivan & Peters. Now, Shumway's firm was nearly twice as big as Sullivan, and insurance defense was the smallest department. And everyone knows that the partners would love to repeat history, to dump the insurance defense business once again. But Shumway wants it, and so it stays.

Greeting me in the corridor, Artemus introduced me to an associate, Ed Filson, who'd written the brief, and the three of us walked into the courtroom. This was the chief judge's room, three times the size of most courtrooms, oak-paneled from floor to ceiling, the black and silver shield of Cook County looming high above the bench. Here lawyers appeared on the morning their cases are assigned for trial, with the luck of drawing a good judge or a bad one hanging heavy in the air. When a case is close to trial, all motions are assigned here, the chief wanting to insure against a backlog, keep things moving along. He hears motions himself only occasionally, though everyone knew, whatever minion was sitting in his stead marched to the cadence called by the chief. The message was clear: let's clear the docket, get these cases tried.

Since ours was the only motion on the call for that afternoon, the courtroom was empty except for the maroon-jacketed clerk sitting to the right of the bench, but a minute later, Hollis Lagatee's entourage came breezing down the aisle: first Harold Barteldt, a young associate, followed by a chunky woman in a serious black suit I didn't know, followed by a court reporter towing her steno machine on wheels, and finally Hollis himself. Just like high Mass: Barteldt could have led in with a crucifix, the woman behind raising the Good Book on high. I knew Barteldt, had been to scores of depositions with him, yet his eyes did not acknowledge mine, skated past like I was the invisible man. He smiled and nodded to Artemus, though, and took a seat at the other table. Then Lagatee sat, looked over. "Artemus?" he nodded. Then he saw me. "Mike!" He got up, strode over.

"Mike," he said, pumping my hand. "How're you getting on?" He gave my shoulder a sympathetic squeeze, and for the first time that day I felt serious pain from last night's knife wound. Now over sauntered Harold Barteldt, suddenly buddy-buddy too, shoulder to shoulder with his boss. "How're you getting on?" he asked, like it was an original thought.

"All rise," the bailiff bawled, and Judge Patrick Walsh swept into the courtroom. *Walsh!*

"Be seated," Walsh said. Both lawyers approached the bench, and I tried to make myself smaller, scooting over, lining up behind Artemus. "Keep in mind I've read your briefs," he said. "I don't think we need to spend a lot of time on this. Mr. Shumway?"

Hollis Lagatee said, "Your Honor, I have a preliminary matter."

"Go ahead," said Judge Walsh.

"We believe we are very close to locating an eyewitness, Judge. We've had an investigator working virtually around the clock, searching for her. We are moving to continue the hearing for two weeks."

"Mr. Shumway?"

"I object, Your Honor. We have a trial set in just over two months. And anyway, we're here strictly on a question of law. The witness has nothing to do with the issues here."

"Mr. Lagatee, this case has been pending for over three years. You have had ample time to locate witnesses. Motion denied. Proceed, Mr. Shumway."

Artemus began. He was an unusually animated speaker, moving through his argument like some weird ballet. Emphasizing some point, he stepped to his left and turned sideways to the bench, his palms turned outward like Jesus on the mount, leaving nothing but clear, cold air between His Honor and Yours Truly. The judge's eyes were fixed on Artemus, though. I slipped back behind him, then remembered: I'm the invisible man. Judge Walsh probably would not take notice of me any more than Harold Barteldt did.

Now Artemus moved sideways again in a grand gesture, and Judge Walsh's eye rested on me like a laser beam. His mind, though, seemed to be on the argument. At that moment Artemus was making little karate chops on his open hand: "Nothing, *nothing* in the law can be more fundamental, Your Honor . . ." The judge's eyes drew into focus. His brow knotted. "Wait a minute," he said, raising a palm to Artemus. Artemus stopped. You could knead the silence like bread dough.

"Mr. Duncavan, what are you doing in my courtroom?" I stood. Before I could say anything, he asked in a higher pitch, "Are you practicing law, Mr. Duncavan?"

I smiled, started to answer, but he interrupted. "If you are practicing law . . ." His voice was louder now, and shaking. He gave it a moment, trying for composure. His face twitched. "I asked you a question, and I'd better get an answer," he demanded, voice now ascending to yet a higher key. "What-are-you-doing-in-my-courtroom?"

"Your Honor, before I explain, may I tell you what a pleasure it is to be here?"

His glare froze. "I advise you, Mr. Duncavan, none of your smart mouth. I asked you a question."

"You did, Your Honor, you certainly did, and I will answer it this way, but I just want to say, only prefatorially of course—preliminarily, if I may—that it is very nice to be here. A treat, I guess you could call it, Your Honor. After all, it isn't every day that . . ."

He sprang to his feet, rage in his eyes.

"I'm observing," I said.

He mulled this over. Then more calmly, "Well, go observe in some other courtroom, Mr. Duncavan. You are not welcome here."

"I am sincerely disappointed to hear that, Your Honor. Sincerely. May I say, if it please the court . . ."

"It does *not* please the court! You have not even been given leave to *address* the court!"

"Well then, may I say that it brings genuine sadness to my heart." Looking up at those mean little eyes, I just couldn't stop myself. "But anyway, I think I'll stay, Judge. Would it be okay if I sat down now?"

"Leave, Duncavan. *Now.*"

I smiled back, not moving.

"Deputy?"

The deputy sheriff swung a nervous face to the judge, back to me again.

"It's a public courtroom, Judge. I believe there are constitutional issues at hand."

"I'm telling you for the last time, *leave.*"

"Sorry, Your Honor. But I think I'll stay."

"Deputy!" he shouted, "You take this man and . . ." As he turned to look at the deputy, he spotted the court reporter tapping away, and his voice caught. He stopped breathing for so long I thought I'd have to climb up there and give him a Heimlich hug. "What are you *doing?*" he screamed. "This is not on the *record!* I told you, *off the record!*" The reporter's hands dropped to her lap. Judge Walsh snatched up the briefs then, stared at them wide-eyed, hands trembling.

"Your Honor . . ." It was Artemus. Lagatee stood next to him with stony-faced detachment, bored even, letting all who cared to know that he was not the least bit scandalized by any of this, may not have even heard any of it. On the other hand, Barteldt sat at the other table with his mouth hanging open, eyes like two full moons. "Your Honor," Artemus said, "may I suggest a brief recess?" His voice soothed, just cordial enough not to be familiar. Everything's okay, no harm here, shit happens, let's take a minute and regroup.

"Five minutes," Judge Walsh said, and stormed off the bench. I caught the deputy sheriff looking at me sideways; he quickly looked away. Then I saw Artemus fixing me with a pleading look.

I said, "I'm sorry. I'll leave," and relief softened his face.

I walked back to my office, full of fond memories for Judge Walsh. Though he did seem not to like me.

Back at my office, waiting for Artemus' call, I thought of dusting, but I really didn't have a dust cloth, so instead I turned my chair around to watch the pedestrian traffic.

Beth used to say that some day I'd procrastinate about death itself, put it off for another week or so. I looked over at her picture smiling back at me. I hadn't talked to her in months. I used to see her now and then, drive out to Sutler's Grove, meet her for lunch. I still marveled at what a good sport she was, considering. Treated me like a favorite cousin. Sometimes she gave me an affectionate peck on the cheek—but that's all.

The first time I picked her up for dinner, I found a note on her screen door: "Come in, I'll be ready in a jiff." As I sat waiting in her living room, the anticipation of seeing her grew unbearable, and when she came into the room she was prettier than I'd ever seen her. I stood awkwardly, willing away an impulse to embrace her. She extended a hand, keeping her distance, but her face bubbled with delight. We went to a little Italian place: dark, red-checkered tablecloths, candles in Chianti bottles. She would pat the back of my hand now and then, the candle flame dancing in her eyes. The talk was intimate, secret fears, secret pleasures, like when we'd just started dating. But nothing of wanting each other. I wanted her desperately, wanted to beg her to give it one more chance. But I didn't. I knew of her Catholic belief, though, that in the eyes of God we were still married. I drove her home, hoping more than anything I'd ever hoped for, that she'd invite me in. On her front porch, I leaned to kiss her mouth and she turned away, offered her cheek. Then she gave me a smile you might give a naughty child, and was gone into the house without even a good night.

I sat in my car in front of her house for a long time, feeling like Lot's wife, unable to move. The crickets chirped. Her porch light threw down shadows on the street. Then the porch light went out, and I sat there in darkness for a long time.

Now staring at her picture I thought, I could drive out Saturday morning, maybe we could have breakfast, and on an impulse I picked up the phone, dialed her number. It rang for a long time. I was about to hang up when a man answered. The second time he said "Hello," I asked for Beth Curling.

"Yes, just a moment." His accent was British, very elegant. "May I tell her who's calling?"

Who was this guy? I gave him my name and waited, trying to picture him. What was he doing in Beth's house? But when Beth came on, she sounded pleased that I called. I told her a little about the investigation for Artemus, asked about her work.

"Mike, it's almost too much. I've got orders coming in from catalogue houses all over the country. I barely have time to breathe."

"Well, why don't you take a breather on Saturday? How about I pick you up for breakfast?"

The sound of muffled voices. Then I heard her say, with what could have been a trace of irritation, "My ex-husband," and she came back on. "I'm sorry Mike, Frederick was talking to me. What were you saying?"

Frederick. Like he was a pal of mine. I wanted to ask, who the hell is Frederick?—especially since Frederick didn't hesitate to ask who *I* was. "I was wondering if I might pick you up for breakfast tomorrow."

"Oh, Mike, I'd love to . . ."

More muffled voices. I waited, dreading the inevitable "but."

She came back. "But—you've got to bring Stapler, I'd really like to see him, okay? What time?"

I told her we'd be there at eight, hung up, and danced a hornpipe across my office, not even caring about the pain in my ankle. Then I sat down, turned my chair around to watch the happy stream of humanity flowing beneath my window. When the phone rang again it was Artemus. He apologized for asking me to leave.

"You didn't ask me to leave, I volunteered. So what happened?"

"We lost. No surprise there, huh, my friend? Listen, in case you're worried, I don't think the judge knew you were with me. I don't think that had anything to do with it."

I wasn't worried. I never thought the motion had a chance in the first place. But just because we lost the motion didn't mean we lost the case. "Look, Artemus, they've still got to convince a jury. They still can't prove how he died." I listened to my phony assurances echo in my own head. Bartodziec sure as hell didn't shoot himself.

"I talked to Hollis afterward," Artemus said. "They've got a lead on their witness, Shavonne Sykes; he thinks his investigator will have her in a week. But get this. Not only did she supposedly complain to Watson about the broken locks, they say she was a witness to the shooting."

"You mean, eyewitness?"

"Not exactly. Hollis was a little vague, but the lady supposedly saw Bartodziec just before, quarreling in the hallway with some guy who dealt drugs out of the vacant apartment. Right after that, she heard the shot."

"Artemus, there were only two tenants on the third floor, Mattie Croyance and Fannie Walker. Fannie Walker is the only one who said she heard the shot."

"I think one said she also heard voices in the hall, just before," Artemus said.

"Fannie Walker. But she never looked out."

"I guess we'll just have to wait and see."

The way things sat, Lagatee's clan could march their

prize witness into the courtroom right in the middle of the trial, and she could still testify. Either way, we were probably going to a jury. And between a grieving widow and a slum landlord, you didn't have to be Sherlock Holmes to deduce which way they'd lean.

Marty Richter called me late that afternoon. "I got you a little information. Seems voodoo's become a bit of a fad in that neighborhood. More like the religion-of-the-hour, I should say. It may be fairly legit, I don't know. There's a store's opened up on Chicago Avenue near Halsted, selling occult paraphernalia—that seems to be the center of it all, or so I'm told. Supposedly they sell a lot of magical shit under the counter, exotic animal bones, powdered monkey pancreas. Aphrodisiacs, and for casting spells and stuff, I guess."

"Jesus. The kind of place that could use a gorilla skeleton, wouldn't you say?"

"Not to mention a whale penis."

"There's got to be a connection, Marty."

"Yeah, a connection to whatever's going on in the basement of that building. But keep your eye on the prize, pal. You want to know why the Polack got wasted. Don't get sidetracked."

"I know."

" 'I know.' That means you'll be dropping by the store, am I right?"

"Can't hurt."

"Thought so. Pick me up something to keep my pecker hard, will ya? Half a pound of dried mink glands, something like that?"

"When was the last time you saw your pecker, Marty?"

"You got good equipment, you keep a roof over it."

"Goodbye."

I put my chin on my fists, teeth vibrating as the el thundered past. The smart thing would be to leave it alone, but I knew that in the end I could no longer leave it alone than I could leave those torn pieces of that lovely lady's note on the sidewalk. I might as well get it over with. I grabbed my straw hat and headed out the door.

I took Milwaukee to Chicago Avenue and headed west, wishing I'd asked him exactly where the store was. Half a mile past Halsted, I made a U-turn, cruising slowly this time. Then I spotted it mid-block, a storefront with a sign, "Occult Happenings." I parked across the street.

Bottles with colored liquids, amulets, dream books, plaster cobras with ruby eyes, an assortment of crystals filled the window. I went in, the door jangling just like an old-fashioned grocery store, the air heavy with the scent of jasmine, here and there thin ribbons of smoke snaking up from incense burning on the counter. At the back a beaded curtain covered the doorway. A black man, his chair tilted back on two legs against the door frame, lowered his newspaper to look at me. Fortyish, rimless glasses, close-cropped hair, starched blue dress shirt with the sleeves rolled up. He took his time folding the paper, then came over and stood behind the counter. "Can I help you?" The accent was West Indies. The smile came late but friendly.

"I'm looking for a deck of tarot cards," I said, wishing I had thought this out before coming in.

"Sure, we got a variety of them." He led me to the back, past a row of plastic skulls with holes in the top and green glass eyes, to a wall of books.

"It's for my daughter," I said. "For school, she's doing a project."

"Really?" He seemed pleased. "We've got a selection, all different prices. I know we used to have one that came with a book, not too expensive. Let's see," he said, scanning a shelf. While he was turned away, I tried peering through the beads to see what was in back of the store. I couldn't see anything. "Here it is." He took it down. *A Beginner's Guide to Tarot.* Twenty-four ninety-five."

"She's also writing about—gosh, I don't know what you'd call it. She says sometimes animal bones are used in ceremonies, or as medicine? And she was wondering if there was any place you could buy things like that."

"Like—" he turned over a hand, prompted with his eyes.

"I don't know. Animal bones, whatever."

He shook his head slowly, smiling as though we were sharing a joke. "Sorry," he said. "You can buy such things in other countries. In Africa, in Haiti, but I've never heard of it in the United States."

"Yeah, well you know, kids." I chuckled lamely. "I gotta give her credit, though. She wants her presentation to be realistic."

"What is her presentation about? Tarot cards and folk medicine, I mean, those are very different things."

"That's what I thought, but I decided I'd let her sort it out herself."

"I'm sorry, I wish I could help," he said.

I paid for the tarot cards and left. Walking back to the car I asked myself: what did I just do, other than spend twenty-five bucks I couldn't afford?

Saturday, August 12

Saturday morning, up early, Stapler and I drove out of the city to Beth's, the cornfields golden in the early sun. Sutler's Grove was a genuine small town, an island amidst fields of grain, though its rural culture had waned, metamorphosing into an artist's colony. I crossed the rusty railroad tracks between faded cross bucks and turned into her shady street. The town consisted of about twenty-five houses, big, old Victorians. There were sidewalks but no curbs, the edges of the lawns giving way to the street's gravel edge. I parked in front of Beth's place, gray with white trim, maroon filigree, red petunias hanging in a couple of baskets on the wide front porch, a white picket fence surrounding all. The small barn in back mirrored the house's paint scheme. The fresh paint and Victorian turrets put you in mind of a theme park.

I mounted the steps, a lawnmower purring in the distance, the smell of freshly-mown hay hanging in the air, and twisted the key in the brass dome on the door. It jangled like an old-time telephone. A guy came to the door, erect, wisps of thinning blond hair swept back, carefully trimmed mustache, horn-rimmed glasses. This would be Frederick. He wore a chambray work shirt and Levi's, both of which had recently been pressed. First impression: Frederick was fastidious, and also unfriendly. He did not introduce himself. He stepped back, appraising Stapler neutrally, pretending to mask his disapproval, and allowed us to enter.

"Beth will be down in a minute. You can have a seat in the living room." As he marched toward the back of the house I was sure he had a poker up his ass. Who was this creep, I wondered, and what was he doing in my wife's house? After all, according to Beth we were still married in the eyes of God.

Beth appeared in the doorway with that jubilant smile of hers, and the little crow's feet around her eyes seemed only to heighten her radiance. She patted her knees to Stapler. He romped over, tried lapping her face, and she pressed his head to her bosom. You know you need therapy when your own dog makes you jealous. Hard to believe there'd been a time she'd have done the same for me. She straightened, still showing that glorious smile, and extended her hand. "He's becoming famous, Mike, that dog of yours. He's my most popular piece in the outdoors line."

We were just leaving when Frederick returned. "Beth, I'll be doing the marketing today. Need anything, dear?"

Marketing? *Dear?* A little show for my benefit, the phony bastard. Beth pressed a finger against her lower lip. "No, but I think you're out of alfalfa sprouts. Better check." She gave a little wave with her finger tips. "Bye-bye."

"What's the matter, Mike?" she asked. We were sitting in a booth next to a window, where we could watch Stapler watch us from the front seat of the Omni.

"Nothing's the matter. Preoccupied with this case, I guess. So. Seen any good movies lately?"

She shook her head slowly, her eyes drilling a hole in my skull. "Mike, you are pouting. You should be ashamed, at your age. Is this about Frederick?"

"No," I said, forcing a laugh. "But since you brought it up, what about Frederick?"

Her eyes searched mine. "What, what about him?"

I turned my hands palms up. "Who is he?"

"He's a painter. He's set up a studio in the barn, up in the loft. The light's good up there, with those big hay mow doors."

"He's living with you?"

She nodded agreeably. "You should see his work, Mike. Midwestern landscapes. Absolutely breathtaking."

"So, then, you and he are . . ." I held out my hand, rocked it a little.

126

"What's that supposed to mean?" She took a forkful of pancake.

"Oh come on, Beth. You know what it's supposed to mean."

She put down her fork, leaned back in the booth. "Mike, Mike, Mike," she said. "We're divorced, did you forget? Shall I recount the ways you were unhappy, being married to me?"

"No, no," I groped. "It's just . . . you always said you believed we were still married in the eyes of God, that's all. I just wondered when that changed."

She laughed so abruptly she snorted, then covered her mouth with her hand. "Sorry. Mike, you're going to be fifty years old. When do you plan on joining the adult world?" Before I could say anything she reached over, put her hand on mine. "I'm sorry. That was cruel." She squeezed my hand, a gesture of sympathy.

"Well, I thought we were having an adult conversation here," I said.

"Right. I do believe that. I take being a Catholic seriously." She fought back a grin. "But I never said I'd spend the rest of my life as a celibate, for God's sake." She laughed then, covered her mouth again. "Sorry." She gave the back of my hand another little pat. I needed to get out of there.

When I dropped her off, she asked if I wanted to come in, but I told her I had to get back to the city, that I should be working on the case every minute. She gave me a smile edged with sadness, and I watched her amble up the walk and disappear into the house without looking back. I had lost Beth years ago; why was this acute pain only now settling in? Better question: why did I give up the best thing in my life? But the real question was the one Beth asked: why couldn't I just grow up, like other people did? My limbs felt like lead. I did not want to move. I put the car in gear, patted the front seat for Stapler, who leaped from the back and settled himself on the passenger's seat. I drove off, loneliness covering me like a monk's hood.

I remembered Danny McGarry's invitation to come out to his house, realized I hadn't called to say I wasn't coming. I got his number from directory assistance, called him on my cell phone. As it rang I drummed my fingers on the steering wheel, wanting very much for him to be there, the quiet between rings seeming like forever. He picked up on the fifth ring. I told him I had just left Beth's, in Sutler's Grove.

"Why don't you come by now?" he said. He gave me directions. Barrington was practically on the way home.

The road was lined on both sides with privacy hedges, the houses mostly invisible from the road, but I counted driveways as instructed. I turned into Danny's, and the house came into view, a modern stone-and-brick ranch, the driveway paralleling a white fence, then angling toward the house. Horses in the pasture across the fence lifted their heads, followed my progress up the blacktop. The place looked to be about three acres, the house fairly modest compared to the neighbors'.

Danny came out, stood grinning next to the car before I shut off the engine. When I opened the door, Stapler leaped over me, stood wagging his tail at Danny.

"What's his name?" he asked, rubbing his scalp.

"Stapler. It's a long story," I said.

"Bring him in." I was glad he offered, since it was getting too hot to leave him in the car.

As we walked to the front door he said, "I'm really delighted you came," and I could tell he meant it, and I sud-

denly felt sorry for him, had the impression he was thirsty
for companionship. He gave me a tour of the house: four
bedrooms, a big kitchen with an island, a formal dining
room, a family room with sliding glass doors leading to the
outdoor pool. It seemed a lot of house for one person. He
was unusually talkative, and though he appeared healthier
than the last time I'd seem him, I was struck for a second
time how thin he looked. Gone was the fat from around his
chin that had given him his jovial, college-boy look.

"You're a long way from Notre Dame," I said.

"I make most of the home games, though."

"You're also a long way from the office. And you're still
doing all that volunteer work." It had seemed to me that
Danny could never say no to any do-good organization
looking for free legal work, always defending some indigent
prisoner for free, or writing an amicus curiae brief for some
liberal cause.

He shook his head. "I've cut back a lot. Did you bring
your swimming trunks?"

"No, I just came from having breakfast with my ex."

"How about a drink, then?" I avoided looking at my
watch, knowing it wasn't even ten-thirty. He seemed a little
jittery, talking louder than he needed to. Before I could answer, he said loudly, "Drinks by the pool, Mike!" his voice
somehow off-key. His eyes seemed not quite focused.

"I'd really like a cup of coffee, if you've got it."

He led me back to the kitchen, put on a pot of coffee,
then we sat at a table next to the pool. After awhile he
seemed to relax, acted more his old self, talked about the
break-up of his marriage.

"I didn't buy the house until after the divorce was final.
Lucky for me, that quad case didn't settle until after we
signed the property settlement. Otherwise, she'd have taken

at least half, and I'd never have gotten this place. Paid cash for it, Mike. My accountant told me I was nuts, but I wanted the place free and clear. What do you think? Bad idea?"

I suddenly wondered if Danny saw me as a father figure. I shrugged. "What do I know?"

"You get along pretty good with your ex, huh?"

"My first wife, yeah. Not my second. That one lasted less than a year. She took about everything I had. Had left, that is."

"Geez, with such a short marriage? It's none of my business, but, hey—as one divorced lawyer to another, how'd she manage that?"

I didn't mind talking about it, I just didn't know where to start. I sat back. "When I got disbarred, she wanted nothing to do with me. Turned ugly, goaded me constantly. I was inadequate in bed, she told me. Funny: humping a successful lawyer turned her into a fucking acrobat. It was the ex-lawyer she couldn't stand. She'd stay out all night, come home in the morning, and tell me how she'd been with some other guy. Or she'd tell me how she loved meeting a stranger in a bar, give him a blow job in the front seat of his car. Or her car. She said either way, it gave her a sense of power. Thing is, at that point I didn't even give a shit. It was her gratuitous malice that got to me. One day I slapped her. Not hard, really. That, I found out later, was the plan. Her lawyer had told her that if I ever hit her, I'd lose my private investigator's license. I couldn't get a concealed carry permit. I wouldn't even be allowed to own a gun. So the deal was simple: she took everything, I kept my license."

"Bummer," said Danny. "Man, oh man." He was looking at the pool, his head wagging from side to side.

"Wow, and I thought my ex was bad." He told me then how he was in a terrible rut himself, hated the bar scene, the meet markets. "But it seems every night after work, I wind up stopping in a bar downtown. Maybe buying this place was a mistake. It's a long way from the Loop, and it's awfully empty when I get home. My mother's pushing me to join the Young Adults Club at her parish." He chuckled. "She thinks I'm still twenty-one."

After the third cup of coffee I asked where the bathroom was. He told me, then said, "Hey, it's time for lunch. Want to go out and grab a bite?"

I said I really had to get going. In the bathroom, as I washed my hands I noticed something, a hand mirror laying on the vanity. Most men I know do not use a hand mirror, but what interested me was something else, something on the surface. I picked it up and looking closer, knew I'd found the probable explanation for Danny's weight loss, as well as his edginess: a tiny residue of white powder.

Chapter Eleven

On the way home I stopped at Fannie Walker's building, rang the bell. Again, nobody home. If it wasn't for bad luck, it seemed I'd have no luck at all. I drove over to Chicago Avenue, parked across the street from Occult Happenings, watched the place for awhile. My shoulder was throbbing and I kept shifting for a comfortable position as I watched the store. Saturday afternoon business was good, customers coming and going. I had no idea what I might see, and after half an hour I left, driving around through the alley first, to get a look at the back. Not much to see, except a green Dumpster squatting near the back door. I wanted to get out and have a look inside—not that I would be conspicuous, of course, some weird white guy in a straw hat getting out of an old rusty Dodge hatchback to pick through the garbage in the ghetto. Hard to believe, there was a time when mail came addressed to me as Mike Duncavan, *Esquire*. I drove home.

But that night I couldn't sleep, wondering what was in that Dumpster, and when the luminous numbers on the clock tripped over to seven minutes past one, I pulled on a pair of Bermuda shorts, slipped on the .357 in a belt holster, covered it with a loose tee shirt, called Stapler, and the two of us set out in the hot night air to go Dumpster-diving. Well, not Stapler. Stapler would be the lookout.

At two a.m. Chicago Avenue still rippled with a fair amount of foot traffic, this being Saturday night. The late bars didn't close until four, and I knew some would still be packed at closing time. I drove past the front of the store to check that the lights were all out and no one was inside. Seeing it was all in darkness I drove around the long way to the back. As I turned into the alley, a huddle of headlight-panicked rats broke apart, scurried in all directions. I pulled up across from the back of the store, the passenger side nearly brushing the wall, maybe eighty feet from the other end of the alley. The street lamp at the corner threw down shadows, and bathed the pavement and buildings in an orange dusk. Nothing moved.

Stapler tried to follow me. "Stay," I told him, and he did, poised on the passenger seat, ears cocked, disdain in his eyes.

Now, I hate rats even more than I hate big hairy spiders and things you see from the corner of your eye, scurrying away on little legs, and I knew the vermin density was high here: rat Calcutta. I switched on my flashlight, scanned around the Dumpster. No rats. But as I approached, the blue-white eye shine of a big one ascended over the edge of the back door steps, reversed course, snaked along the edge of the building and into a crevice. When I was sure it was gone, I went to the Dumpster, swung the lid open. It fell backward with a crash like a gunshot. I froze, stood watching to see what kind of attention I'd drawn, as a liquid stench surging out of the Dumpster surrounded me.

When I was sure no one had taken notice, I probed the flashlight's beam around the interior of the Dumpster. At one end, trembling with maggots, lay the carcasses of three dead cats, bellies sliced open, eviscerated, tops of the heads neatly sawed off, brains scooped out. There was also a pile of old newspapers, and what looked like the emptied contents of an office waste basket. I put my hands on the rim as far away from the dead cats as I could get, swung my belly onto the edge and hung down inside, then as I pawed

133

through the dry trash, the layer of stench grew so foul I started to retch. I concentrated on breathing through my mouth, quickly poked through what was there: discarded catalogues, crumpled stationery, shavings from a pencil sharpener, an empty bottle of White Out, wrappings from a Big Mac. I grabbed a yellow legal pad, a page torn from a desk-sized calendar, and climbed out.

Then I saw I had company, a black guy in his early twenties just inside the mouth of the alley, standing behind a telephone pole. Giving his dick a final shake. He looked at me over his shoulder and yelled, "Hey, yo!" and walked quickly toward me. Three seconds later, two more guys came around the corner.

"The fuck you doin' man," the first one demanded, and as they circled me, a second one said, "Got any money, man?"

Without waiting for an answer, the first one said, "Better give it up, man. Give us your money now, you want to live."

I transferred the stuff I was carrying to my left hand, freeing my gun hand. "How 'bout you come and get it?" I said.

A moment of uncertainty flickered in Number One's eye. "Wait a minute," he said, but the second was grinning now, eyeing my Bermuda shorts.

"What? Say, ain't he got some pretty legs, though?" They all hooted.

I looked the first one dead in the eye. "Your friend here likes my legs? Tell me, is this weenie some kind of a dick licker?"

"What?" Sparks in his eyes, Number Two took a step toward me. "Nigger, who you callin' a dick licker?"

I wanted to tell him I was shocked and offended by the

N word, but the first one snatched his arm and, without taking his eyes off me, said, "Whoa, wait a minute. Say, you real slick, you know that? You deep undercover, huh, wearin' that silly-ass straw hat?" He snickered. "What you 'posed to look like, some wino goin' through the trash?" The other two laughed.

I laughed too, trying to keep cool, but they were pissing me off. I stepped between them, elbowing the .357 forward on my belt for an easier reach, and walked over to my car, then catching sight of Stapler's thrashing tail, I was afraid if I opened the door he'd jump out and try to make friends.

"Think we don't know your sorry-ass gig, man?" the first one said. "Where yo' backup at?" He spun and walked back toward the mouth of alley, looking to left and right, came back. "I know they out there somewhere."

"Backup? Ain't nothing here but pussies and dick lickers, what would I want with backup?" It was probably not a real adult thing to say; as I said, they were pissing me off. "Besides, you got it wrong. I'm not a policeman."

"Pussies? Who the *fuck* you calling pussies, nigger?" Number Two started for me, more in earnest this time, but Number One grabbed his arm again. "Hold it, hold it, *hold it,* man, you bein' set up, don't you see that?"

"Who you callin' nigger, pussy?" I said.

Number One scowled at me. "Muthuhfuckin' crime, way y'all do people." He turned to his pal. "Look, this pig gonna say somethin' into his armpit and bam! Muthuhfuckahs come out the walls, man, stomp yo ass into Jell-O. They done me that way once, man, I ain't gonna fall for it again. It's sickening, man, the way they do."

"You got it wrong, I'm not a policeman," I said. I was really pissed now, and my motives were dark. "Really, no shit. I'm not the police."

"So what's that bulge under your shirt? A spare ass?"

The two howled, but the one who had been silent just shook his head. "That's some sneaky shit, man," he said. "Some wrong shit."

"Entrapment," said Number Two.

"Entrapment, right, that's what it is," said Number One.

"Good night, gentlemen," I said. I opened the door just enough to shove Stapler onto the passenger seat and squeeze in.

"Man, he even got him a dog," one of them said.

"What the muthahfuckahs won't do."

"Sickening."

I turned onto Elston Avenue, hands trembling on the steering wheel. It wasn't fear, it was adrenaline. Buck fever. It had not been a particularly courageous act, since at no time did I feel vulnerable, at every instant sure I would sense the subtle line-crossing, the committed gesture, and react: draw and shoot three men in less than three seconds. Moves I'd practiced time and again, on silhouette targets on the range, on buckets swung from a tree, until my trigger finger throbbed and the web of my gun hand smarted. Had that confidence wavered even slightly, I would have been scared silly. Was it overconfidence? The question was not new; my brain said probably, but the answer never seemed to reach my gut.

But there was another question whose answer was less certain. If it had gone down, what then? Call the police, allow the survivors (if any) to press charges against me? Leave my entire life in the hands of a jury? Or leave the dirt bags lying in the alley, and scan the papers the following morning for any news. My brain said probably the latter, but of this I was less sure.

At home I poured myself a drink, pulled out a chair, and

sat at the kitchen table to look over the legal pad and the calendar, but after a minute the stench of the Dumpster seemed to hang in my face. I took one gulp of vodka, then stripped off my clothes and took a shower. When I sat down again the smell was still there, and I realized that of course it was coming from those treasures out of the garbage. I flipped through the pad's yellow pages, anxious to be done with it and get it out of my house. On every page were columns of figures, the margins filled with a variety of doodles, spirals, squares within squares, faces in profile, stick horses. But on one page was a list of names, with no heading. My eye ran down the list, then again. Just names I didn't know.

I looked over at the calendar page, saw several of the same names written there with phone numbers. And then my pulse quickened. I looked away, wanting to be sure, then back. Under Thursday, June 8th, was a notation: "Gorilla bones. Mattie Croyance, 773-555-5749."

So Watson's former third-floor tenant was involved in the late night rituals at the building—a connection was clicking into place. From the wall phone in the kitchen, I dialed the cross-listing service, hoping to get an address from the phone number, but all I got was that mechanical message: "We're sorry. At the customer's request, the information you have requested is not listed."

At three-thirty in the morning, I resisted the temptation to dial the number. Though she'd probably been breaking into Moses' building, no good would come of pissing her off, at least not until I knew where she fit into this picture. And she hadn't broken in, exactly, she apparently had a key. The locks had all been changed since the fire, so it wasn't a key left over from when she lived there. Where did she get it? That was not a question she was likely to answer. Even so, I was feeling pretty good, until I remembered how many days I had left. This was a long way from a connection to Bartodziec's death.

I sat there, spirits stalled and too keyed up to sleep, and drank two more drinks. Then I spotted the package laying on the radiator in the dining room, the deck of tarot cards and the introductory book. I poured myself one more, brought it over to the kitchen table. I tore off the cellophane, and tried to throw it in the waste basket, but it stuck to the back of my hand. I shook it. Then I shook it again. It did not let go. An omen? With the other hand I crumpled it into a ball, threw it in the waste basket, and picked up the deck. I had no idea what I was doing, but what the hell? I shuffled, then dealt myself five cards face down in a line. I stared at the card backs, sipping at my vodka. So what do they have to say about Mike? I reached to turn one over, my hand hovering over the farthest one on the left. But in what order should they be turned over? Since it's supposed to be arcane, I decided to do it backwards. I placed a hand on the right end card, took a slug of my drink with the other.

"Tell me the truth," I said aloud, "or I'll turn you in for a Ouija board." At the sound of my voice Stapler got up, came over, nuzzled his nose under my hand. I turned the card over.

The Fool. A confident young man in mid-stride, eyes to the heavens, bag on a stick over his shoulder like a hobo, about to step off a cliff. He happened to be accompanied by a dog. I turned over the next one.

The Hermit. Head bowed and cowled like a monk's, leaning on his staff, holding a lantern in his extended hand. Next.

The Hanged Man. Dangling upside down, eyes staring.

Enough of this. I picked up the cards and returned them to the deck, but sat scrutinizing the neat stack on the table.

"Here's what we'll do, Stapler." I shuffled the deck. He thumped his tail. "This one will be Danny McGarry. And this is Artemus Shumway." I dealt the two face down, guzzled the dregs of my glass, went to the freezer for fresh ice cubes, poured a refill, took a long slug.

"He-e-e-e-re's Danny!" I said, and reached for the card on the left, turned it over. The Magician: long, white beard, cone-shaped hat, head wreathed in stars, wand raised on high, the elements arrayed on a table before him.

"Hah! What'd I tell you, Stapes? Fake! Now for *Artemus.*" I turned over the last card. Six of pentacles. A reclining, seductive woman, a man seated on the floor next to her, holding her hand. "Charity," the caption read. What did this seductive creature have to do with charity? I reached for the book, located the card's explanation.

"In the ancient Gnostic gospels, it was the whore, not the clergyman, who was the chief dispenser of charity. She symbolizes the spirit of kindness and loving, an image which may devolve from Mary Magdalene, or from a much earlier figure, the promiscuous goddess of the Greek temple. An archetype for feminine caring."

Well, it had nothing to do with Artemus. Remembering my first card, I found The Fool in the chapter, "How to Read the Cards":

"You are out of sync with the world, isolated, yet perhaps headstrong. Your current situation may differ from those around you, which may cause you to feel you are 'marching to a different drummer.' You need to pay attention to the drumbeat you are hearing; it is your authentic self, trying to get your attention."

I closed the book, then, as I reached to pick up the cards that were Danny and Artemus, I realized that I had reversed them.

* * * * *

Sunday, August 13

I caught Mass at Old St. Patrick's. I go there mainly for Father Jack Wall's sermons, but as I knelt near the back I noticed for the first time that the congregation was made up almost entirely of couples. Afterward, as Father Wall greeted the faithful two by two in front of the church, I left by a side door.

All afternoon I kept trying to call Mattie Croyance. There was no answer, but at least it seemed to be a working number. In the afternoon I drove over to Lincoln Park with Stapler, took him for a long walk, came home, and watched *Sixty Minutes*. Afterward, I tried the number again. This time, Mattie Croyance answered.

I told her I represented Moses Watson, that I was calling about the man who'd been shot in the hallway of his building. "Would you mind if I came by and asked you a few questions?"

"What do you want to know?" She had a thick Haitian accent, and her manner was suspicious. It should have been.

"It would be easier if I could come by and talk to you in person. It'll only take a few minutes."

"I told the police everyt'ing I know."

"Do you mind if I come by?"

"No, don't want to talk to you. I tol' the police, I saw nothing."

"But you heard shots?"

"No, I didn't see anyt'ing, I didn't hear anyt'ing."

"Ms. Croyance, was your daughter there at the time?"

There was silence for about five seconds. "Yes, I t'ink she was. It was a long time ago. Look, I got to go."

"Ms. Croyance, why didn't you tell the police that your daughter was home? You never mentioned your daughter."

"Listen Mr.—what did you say your name was?"

"Duncavan."

"Did the police ask me if my daughter was home, Mr. Duncavan?" Without waiting for an answer, she said, "Maybe they just did not write that down. I don't remember, it was a long time ago. I'm sorry, I cannot talk to you any longer, I mus' go now."

"Wait. Look, I know you've been going back to the building at night. I know about the stolen bones. Tell me, who let you in?"

The line went dead.

Monday, August 14

I woke up Monday morning feeling punk, a little clammy. I pulled on my brown oxfords, noting that I should not go one more day without a shine. Then as I fought traffic on the Kennedy into the Loop, the three would-be muggers disturbed me, the near miss on Saturday night; how sometimes violence will pass over you like the shadow of a buzzard's wing, and be gone. I thought of this, not knowing that within a few hours violence would visit me again, not quite passing by this time.

I pulled into the parking garage, debating whether to walk over to City Hall for a shoe shine. It was still early, and not sure what time the stand opened, I went up to the office. I picked up the phone before making coffee, called the Property Crimes section at Area One, asked for the detective who'd investigated the burglary at the Adventurer's Club.

He came on in less than ten seconds. "Detective Kinnane."

141

"Mike Duncavan, Detective. I've got some information you maybe could use. I'm working for the guy who owns the building where the Adventurer's Club stuff was recovered, and—"

"You the guy found the gorilla bones and stuff?"

I braced myself. "Right."

"Listen, you made those adventurer guys real happy. Let me tell you, no way could you put a price on that stuff. Irreplaceable, been in their club forever. Some of those artifacts were donated by famous explorers, back to the nineteenth century."

"Well, here's a lead on who took it." I told him about Occult Happenings, finding Mattie's name with the "gorilla bones" notation on the calendar.

Before I said goodbye, he asked, "You mean you actually climbed in the Dumpster?"

I had just finished making coffee when the phone started ringing, and I poured a cup, wiped my hands on a paper towel, took it to my desk, and got it on the fourth ring. It was Artemus, with some depressing news. "Mike, Lagatee's investigator found their key witness, Shavonne Sykes. They've faxed me her affidavit. I'm taking her deposition tomorrow. Want to be there?"

"Sure. Does it by any chance say what apartment she lived in?"

"Good point. Hang on, I don't have it in my hand." I sipped the coffee, wiped a ring off my desk with my wrist, set the cup back down. He came back in thirty seconds. "She says, apartment 3 South."

"That was Mattie Croyance's apartment," I said. "Moses said Mattie lived alone."

"I know, and the night of the shooting she told the police she didn't hear anything, right?"

"Right. And she never said anything about anyone else being there. Listen, Artemus, I've found out something else. Mattie Croyance is connected somehow to the break-ins at the building, the voodoo stuff." I told him about the information I'd recovered from the Dumpster. He listened politely; he did not seem impressed.

"Interesting," he said, without enthusiasm. "You said break-ins. But didn't you say you thought someone was using a key?"

"Right, but that's another thing. Where the hell did they get a key?"

For a second I thought we were disconnected. Then Artemus said, "You know that sounds like some good detective work, Mike, but I'm not sure what it has to do with the murder. Doesn't Moses Watson have another lawyer to look after the building matters?"

"Yeah. Danny McGarry. You know Danny?"

"Can't say I do," he said. The next silence gave me the impression that Artemus wasn't pleased. "Mike, God knows I don't want to tell you how to do your job, but—we haven't got much time. Maybe you should be concentrating on finding out something about the murder. Let the other lawyer worry about what's going on in the building."

I lifted my feet onto the desk and leaned back, wanting to tell him I was following my gut, which is what he'd hired me to do. But I didn't. I studied the scuffed toes of my brogans, not even sure, at this point, if I should be all that confident in my gut. "Fax me the affidavit, okay?" I asked him.

I hung up and headed over to the shoe shine stand at City Hall. I didn't know the fellow's name, but he gave the best shine in town. There were two guys there ahead of me, sitting up on the bench in the orange jackets and big plastic badges of commodities traders, chewing on fat cigars. I picked up the *Sun Times* from the empty seat, climbed up next to them, immersed myself in the business section. They were laughing a lot, entertaining each other. Then one of them said, "Pop that rag, boy!" Maybe you had to be drunk from an early lunch, but that caused the other to convulse with laughter. I looked over the top of my paper. The shoe shine man kept his head down, kept working. Now once you've told a joke, it's usually not funny a second time. Unless maybe you add a new wrinkle.

"Pop that rag, boy!" the closest one said again. This time he held out his cigar in a bad imitation of Groucho Marx and popped the ashes onto the man's head. The second one broke up all over again.

I turned to the one next to me, said very calmly, "Time to leave."

He looked at me, puzzled. "What?" He jabbed the cigar back into his mouth and smirked. He had a beer gut, and a couple of extra chins hanging under his jaw.

"I said, it's time to go now. You're finished here. Pay the man."

Then the shoe shine man turned his face up to me. "Please, I don't want no trouble."

The fat one removed the cigar. "Who the fuck are you, asshole?" He looked over his shoulder at his pal and gave a sharp, falsetto laugh.

His pal laughed too, and decided to make his own joke. "Say, who gave you that straw hat? Your grandpa?" He laughed like a bird chirping.

Not to be upstaged, the fat one didn't laugh. He looked at me deadpan and said, "Have some respect, Ern, this guy *is* someone's grandpa."

I spun, powering with my legs, rammed the web of my

hand up into his throat, banged his head against the wall, and pinned him there. His hands wrapped around mine, prying at my grip, eyes bulging, panicky, making little choking sounds, dancing like a fish at the end of a line, and then his friend grabbed my wrist, too, started screaming, "Let him go, for Christ sake, let go." But my elbow was locked up, my arm trembling, and I held on, his carotids pulsing at my fingertips. I squeezed them together, watched his eyes roll back. Then I heard the shoe shine man yelling, "Let him go, mister, please. Let him go!" I did. His ass hit the seat hard, and his hands went to his neck, and he sat there bent over, croaking, sucking in gallons of air. I looked around. A small crowd had gathered. There were always cops around City Hall, so I decided against getting a shine after all. I got down, gave the man a five-dollar bill, and walked back to my office, my arm trembling and sore. I started feeling clammy all over, a little nauseated, thought I might be coming down with the flu, and maybe the effort aggravated it. I was not feeling real happy with myself, either, thinking there might have been a better way to handle it. I wondered if there was some kind of twelve-step program for people like me.

Back in the office I found Shavonne Sykes' affidavit in the fax machine, and when I sat at my desk to read it, my arm was still shaking. According to the affidavit, Shavonne had complained to Moses Watson several times about the broken lock on the front door. She told him strangers were coming into the building, harassing tenants at all hours. Homeless people, loitering in the hallways, would ask her for money, and when she refused, they'd threaten her. At the time of the shooting, apartment 2 South had been vacant. Drug dealers had broken in, and were selling drugs out of there.

Shavonne Sykes' testimony would establish that Moses Watson had notice of the broken locks in the vestibule, which resulted in crimes being committed in the building. Her testimony would get the plaintiff's case to the jury. It said nothing about what she did that night, in response to the shooting. Lagatee probably wanted to show he could prove the notice issue—that Watson knew about the broken locks and did nothing about it—and make Artemus work for what he needed; he'd have his chance at the deposition. Fannie Walker, across the hall, said she'd called the police—did Shavonne call, too? If she said she did, it was doubtful we could prove otherwise. The tapes at the police communications center would have been destroyed long ago. But Shavonne wasn't listed anywhere on the police reports, even though her mother had been interviewed. And her mother said she'd heard nothing, and never mentioned Shavonne. I needed to talk to Detective Bertucci again. I also needed to talk to Fannie Walker. In my gut, I knew Shavonne Sykes was lying.

First, though, I called Moses Watson to confirm what he'd told me, that Sykes wasn't living in that apartment.

"Mattie Croyance lived alone," he said. "No one else lived there."

"You're sure?" I asked.

"I'm positive."

"Could she maybe have lived there without your knowing?"

He hesitated. "Don't see how. I lived on the first floor."

I wished I had a stronger witness than Moses to testify that Shavonne Sykes didn't live in the building, someone with no self-interest. I made a note to call Robert Norton again. I had forgotten to ask him about Sykes.

I dug out the police reports once more. Bertucci's first

146

report, the one covering his investigation on the night of the shooting, showed that he'd spoken to Mattie Croyance, a tenant in 3 South. She said she had not seen or heard anything.

I dialed Area Three headquarters, luckily caught Bertucci in the office. He said he was catching up on paperwork, and agreed to see me. I drove over, bringing along all the case reports. We sat across from each other at a gray metal table in an interrogation room. Bertucci studied the reports for a long time without saying anything. When he put them down, he said, "I kind of remember. A middle-aged woman on the third floor, yeah. It's like I said in the report. She heard shots, but that was all."

"Do you recall if she said anything about anyone else being there?"

"No, but I would have asked her that. If there was anyone else, I would have noted it in my report. And I would have tried to interview them."

I thanked Detective Bertucci, and as I left I was surprised to find myself moving in a sort of nostalgic fog. The headquarters building for Area Three was brand new, with amenities we never dreamed of when I was a policeman. Yet the atmosphere was unchanged, the sense you were living a little on the edge, the spark of adventure. I would have left the department anyway, once I graduated from law school. I only wished the memory could be a wholesome one, unstained by the disgrace of my departure. Better that the violent moment which brought my police career to a close had ended in my death, and not that of an innocent.

Chapter Twelve

Innocent is how I still picture them, that night I met Henry and Patricia. I had recently transferred from the detective division back to patrol, which was more compatible with law school classes. They lived in a house on my beat, in Hyde Park. In the small hours of the morning, I responded to their call, joined by another officer from another beat. They had been awakened by strange noises and, aware of a rash of house burglaries in the neighborhood, were convinced that an intruder was in the house. I interviewed them, both a little shaken, standing in the living room in their night clothes, unaware that they had opened their door to an interloper far more sinister than any burglar. Henry seemed frail and geeky, the kind of guy you instinctively wanted to protect. Patricia's loose cotton nightgown could not hide the fullness of her young breasts, the seductive curve of her hips. Nor did it deter my thoughts of her nakedness underneath.

We made a thorough search of the house, checked all around the exterior for any signs of forced entry. It was secure; there was no burglar. The other officer left. Then Henry said he could not go back to sleep, and asked if I would like some coffee, and we sat at the kitchen table, the three of us, getting to know each other. She was a grade school teacher at a school in Hyde Park, he was doing postdoctoral research in microbiology at the University of Chicago. I could tell they both liked me, probably saw me as a curiosity—an intellectual cop. Henry talked earnestly about his work with viruses. His enthusiasm was infectious, and I nodded at appropriate times, though I never really got a grip on what he was talking about. He told me he had to be in the lab at certain stages in the growth of the virus, which often meant being there all night. He said he worried about Patricia being alone in the house. A little awkwardly, he wondered if it would be too much to ask—could I look in on her now and then?

So self-delusional was I that, when I said it was just part of my job, I actually believed myself—I really thought I was being noble. I could have passed a polygraph, my true motives smothered under layers of rationalization. When I left, Henry was happy; he'd found a friend. He said he'd leave the porch light on when he was going to the lab, so I would know when he wasn't there.

And I said, "Thank you, Henry."

Even so, looking back, I believe that it started innocently. I'd check the house every night, front and back, shine the spotlight along the side, drive around to the alley, walk into the darkened yard. At first, I don't think Patricia even knew I was there. One night, though, a light was burning in the kitchen, and when I flashed the spotlight on the back of the house, she came to the window. When I went into the yard, she asked me to come in.

She couldn't sleep, she said, and was having a cup of tea. Would I like a cup? I started drinking tea that night. We sat at the kitchen table for a long time, sharing too many private thoughts. It should have told me where this was going. But she was religious, a born-again Christian. I thought she felt safe with me, and I put no moves on her.

The next night I went straight to her house from roll call. The porch light was on again, and so was the one in the kitchen. This time, we talked even longer. But when she got up to go to the stove, she didn't sit back down. She laid a hand against my cheek, bent and kissed me on the mouth, a deep, probing kiss. Her robe fell open, exposing a pink nipple. The fruit of the tree of knowledge of good and evil.

We did it on the kitchen table that night. The following night, she took me to her bed. But on the third night the porch light was not burning. Then in the dawn's early light, I saw the two of them leaving for work. Henry spotted me cruising past, flagged me down.

"Mike," he said, "I don't know how I can thank you for looking after Patricia." He reached in the open window, shook my hand. "You're a true Christian," he said. "And a good friend to us."

And I had the balls to say, "I'm just doing my job, Henry."

The next night, Friday, there must have been a full moon. From the minute I got in the car, the radio was jumping, and I raced from one call to another. Things didn't slow down until about three a.m. Then I headed for the house, flicking off the headlights before turning into the alley. Several houses in, there was a car parked in the shadows, engine running, lights off. I pulled up behind it, and as I jotted down the plate number, the car suddenly pulled away in a screech of tires, fish-tailing down the alley. I did not give chase. I called for backup, pretty sure what I had, gave the description of the car and the license number to the dispatcher.

Afraid the burglar might be alerted, I didn't wait for backup. I asked the dispatcher to find the residents' phone number, call and alert them that I was there, not wanting to get shot for a burglar myself. From the top of the basement stairs, I saw that the basement door had been forced open. I went in, probed the corners with my flashlight. Near the back I found him, trying to hide under a pile of laundry. He did not resist.

As I handcuffed him, another car called over the radio that he'd spotted the getaway vehicle speeding down 55th Street, and I followed the progress of the chase as I walked the prisoner back to my squad car. Minutes later, they had the driver in custody, too.

The rash of residential burglaries in Hyde Park came to an end. I was feeling pretty good about myself—I had ended a whole fucking crime wave. Here was proof that my attention to the home of Henry and Patricia had been nobly motivated. I actually believed it.

Henry believed it even more. A couple days later, he'd left a message at the station to call him. "Mike, we are so indebted to you," he said. "Patricia and I would like to take you and your wife out to dinner." When I hesitated, he put Patricia on.

"Come on, we want to meet Beth. It'll be fun," she said.

Beth and I joined Henry and Patricia for dinner. Later, getting ready for bed, Beth said, "I had a nice time, such nice people." We made love that night. In the darkness, Beth became Patricia.

My shift rotated. I started working afternoons, four to midnight, going by the house every night at about eleven p.m. Across the street were twin condominium buildings, California-style, with a courtyard between them. Now when I saw the porch light on, I parked the car behind the condominiums, out of sight. I'd walk through the enclosed stairwell, across the courtyard, then across the street to Henry and Patricia's. But one night, after visiting Patricia, Henry surprised us, coming in as I was leaving. He seemed pleased to see me. "Where's your squad car, Mike?" he asked. "I didn't see it."

I tried to make a joke. "Oh, it's out there somewhere," I

151

said. A bundle of laughs.

The next day I reached Patricia at school, and told her we had to stop, it was too dangerous. She said I was worrying for nothing. Then one night a couple of weeks later, Henry again came home unexpectedly. Patricia and I were standing in the kitchen. This time, he did not seem pleased to see me.

For the next week, I did not see Patricia, but the following week it started again. And again, Henry surprised us. Again, we were standing in the kitchen.

"I was having a cup of tea when Mike shined his light, and I asked him to join me," Patricia said brightly. "Can I get you a cup?" Henry shook his head. He did not smile.

After that night, I stopped going there. The shift changed again. It was summer, I had no law school classes, so I started working days. One morning I saw Henry walking down Woodlawn, and pulled over to say hello. He said hello back without looking at me.

The following week I drove past Patricia's school at recess, saw her in the schoolyard. I wanted to put an end to it, face-to-face, a moment of finality. We talked across the iron fence. She said she missed me. I told her I was sure that Henry knew.

"Nonsense," she said. "He has a lot on his mind. Henry thinks you're a true-life hero." Her eyes drifted to my crotch and back again. "So do I." She smiled wickedly. "Henry's in New York, at a convention. He won't be back until Saturday. I'll be alone, all night." Her eyes lingered.

"I've got to go," she said finally, and walked away, confident I'd come, left me standing there. I did come. I returned every night that week, telling Beth I was going to the law library at the University, which happened to be open until midnight.

The watch changed again, and I was back on the midnight shift, cruising my beat, but the porch light never came on. Then one evening after roll call, as I was passing the front desk, the sergeant said I had a call. It was Patricia.

"Please come by tomorrow night," she said. "I'll be alone again."

"No, I can't," I said. "I'm off tomorrow."

"All the better," she said.

All the following day and into the evening, I told myself I would not go. Then at ten o'clock, I gathered my law books. "I'm going over to the law library," I said.

"You've sure been spending a lot of time at the library," she said as I went out the door.

I drove to Patricia's block and parked in the alley across from her house, behind the condos. I got out of the car, shrugging off a creeping sense of doom, that something was very wrong. Of course something was wrong. I was an adulterer, porking the wife of a man who had called me his friend, sneaking around like a skunk in the night, and lying to my beautiful wife.

I turned into the enclosed stairwell heading for the courtyard, and suddenly a man in dark clothing and a ski mask appeared in front of me, a revolver in his hand, and started shooting. A bullet tore through my side as I snatched my revolver, nearly blinded by the muzzle flashes, and I got off four quick shots at point-blank range before a second bullet ripped through my ankle and sent me sprawling. When I looked up, the guy was lying flat on his back, staring upward. I wanted to shoot the sonofabitch again, but I knew he was dead.

I crawled up next to him, pulled off the ski mask, and saw that it was Henry. I'd put four into a neat group in the center of his chest. You just don't get any deader. I wanted

153

to think that, had I known it was him, I would have stood there and took what I had coming. But you can't change history. Come to think of it, though, I sure changed Henry's. And Patricia's. And Beth's. And mine. When I got to the emergency room that night, they shot me full of morphine, thinking the ankle wound, which nearly took my foot off, was the reason for my uncontrollable weeping.

In the investigation that followed, it came out that Henry had overheard Patricia's call to me the night before. Already suspicious, he'd waited until the next day to confront her. She confessed to him that I had seduced her, and told him that I had been stalking her ever since. She told him she'd asked me to come by only so she could tell me face-to-face, once and for all, to leave her alone, or she'd have my job.

Well, the job was gone, anyway. But at least there were no criminal charges. Sordid as the whole thing was, it was still self-defense. It was another matter with the bar association's Character and Fitness Committee; in the end, they decided I'd only been guilty of adultery, and declined to cast stones.

Chapter Thirteen

Tuesday, August 15

I awoke the following morning feeling a little better, but after forty-five minutes with the free weights I was starting to feel out of sorts, then after just a few minutes of punching the heavy bag I quit, wishing I could take half a bottle of Nyquil and go back to bed. But there were only seven days left, and I sure hadn't made much progress.

When I reached my office, a manila envelope from Artemus was stuffed in the mail slot, copies of the CPD crime lab file he'd received in response to a subpoena. I called Marty Richter, asked him if he'd get Shavonne Sykes' arrest record for me.

"Cost you one martini. Beefeater's, very dry—"

"I know, shaken, not stirred. Have you given any thought to AA?" I gave him her Social Security number and date of birth from the amended answers to interrogatories.

When I hung up, my shoulder was throbbing like an abscessed tooth. I had changed the dressing a few times, tried to put Bacitracin on it, but it was hard to reach, and I could only tape the top of it. It had turned an angry purple and red and was oozing nasty fluid. I made a mental note to make a doctor's appointment.

I opened the envelope with the crime lab reports. There was an inventory form listing what had been recovered (not much); an analysis of scrapings from under Bartodziec's fingernails (nothing useful); photographs of the empty shell casings recovered at the scene; and magnification photographs of the extractor marks and firing pin impression. The markings on the casings were distinctive enough for comparison, but not much good unless you had an exemplar to compare it to.

At five o'clock that afternoon I was feeling like a pile of warm, steaming doo-doo, and my shoulder hurt so bad I couldn't even sit back in my chair. There was just enough time to call, pick one: (a) the doctor's office, or (b) Marie Galkowska. I dug out the piece of paper with Marie's phone numbers from my wallet, dialed her work number.

I recognized the precise, official greeting as Marie's voice, and in that instant some connection flashed in the back of my head, then was lost with the swelling of my crotch and Little Willy's primordial memory. When I told her it was me, her tone was pleasant but distant. She did not seem eager to rip my clothes off. She did ask, "How is your shoulder?"

"Look, why don't I pick you up for dinner and I'll tell you about it?"

Pregnant pause. "I'm sorry, Mike, but I can't."

"Well, it's really hard to change the dressing by myself," said I. "I wish I knew someone who'd give me a hand."

"Mike, look. You are a really sweet guy. I like you, but I can't see you again. That's it."

I did not let on that she had sent my hopes dashing over a cliff. "Uh-huh," I said. "But it's only dinner."

"I can't."

"I won't even touch you, I promise."

"I can't, Mike."

There was a tone of finality, of resolution, so different from that night, and I had a hunch what it was about. "Marie, tell me you haven't gone back with that creep."

Another pregnant pause. "He's not a creep."

156

"He's a creep, you said yourself he was a creep."

"Don't call him a creep. And besides, it's none of your business. I have to say goodbye now, Mike."

"Marie . . ."

"Goodbye." And she was gone. I was still holding the phone when the dial tone came on. I considered calling her back, decided against it. And Beth said I hadn't grown up yet. Thinking I might still reach the doctor's office, I found the number and dialed, got a recorded message: "The office is now closed. If this is an emergency please call . . ."

I replaced the handset and sat heavily in my chair for a moment, my butt feeling like a couple of sandbags. Fighting a creeping sense of doom, I got to my feet, retrieved the Bartodziec file from the credenza, stuffed the crime lab documents inside, and sat down again, gazing at the telephone, thinking how I was unconnected to anyone, how it did not matter to a single soul whether I was going to be late for dinner, or whether I ever ate dinner again. It occurred to me that if I bought the big one right then, checked out at that second, I did not know who would notice my absence. Who cared? Stapler was waiting for me at home, true, along with a freezer full of Hungry Man dinners. I thought then of Danny McGarry, who was no doubt at the moment ensconced in some local after-work meeting place, engaged in repartee with a female whom he would later describe as vacuous. Boring, mind-numbing repartee, he would call it. But it was repartee, nevertheless. A connection with another human being—and, Lord help me, one with tits.

I dialed his number on an impulse, hoping he might still be there, hoping, I suppose, for an invitation to come along to that noisy, dismal world where at least there was light and sound and connection with other people. I got Danny's answering machine; gone for the day. After a moment's reflection I actually felt relieved, remembering that he was fifteen years younger. Probably the looks I'd get from those beauties at the bar, vacuous or not, would only make me feel older. I was feeling like a lone glove lying on the sidewalk.

Absently I picked up the Bartodziec file again, pulled out the investigation folder, and the photocopies of Bartodziec's greeting cards and letters slipped out, fell to the floor. I sat for a moment looking down at them spread at my feet, in the blackness of my mood seeming all the more pathetic, the manicured fingers holding each warm sentiment to the copy machine glass like the cold hand of a grave digger. I bent to pick them up, and it hit me like a right cross to the temple. Still bent, I studied the photocopy of a handwritten note in Polish, then snatched it up, laid it on my desk. Why didn't I notice it sooner? In most of the photos the fingers were curled under, showing the long fingernails, the rhinestone insets, just like Marie's. But on this one, a handwritten letter held palm down, the operator's wrist extended beyond the margin of the paper. I studied it, not quite believing what I saw—a narrow, faint scar running transversely across the wrist. It could not be a coincidence. It was the hand of Marie Galkowska.

I riffled through the folder, snatched out Moses Watson's insurance policy, turned to the declaration page. There it was, in the upper left hand corner: Red Eagle Associates, 4499 N. Milwaukee Avenue, Chicago, IL 60645—an address about two blocks away from Wanda's tavern. I was pretty sure Marie had never told me the name of the agency she worked for, but I was positive that she'd answered the phone with that name. I dialed her number again, got a recorded message: "You have reached Red Eagle Associates. Our office is now closed. If you are . . ."

I hung up, went to the outer office, and paced. What could it mean? What was Marie's connection? Did she know I was investigating Bartodziec's murder? Was that why she wouldn't see me?

I tried calling Moses, wanting to know how he happened to buy his insurance from Red Eagle, but there was no answer, and Moses did not have an answering machine.

My thoughts racing, I decided a drink was in order and headed out to Monk's Pub. It was only two blocks away, but walking over I began feeling clammy all over. I ordered a double Stoli at the bar and sipped, hoping to slow down my brain, ease the sorting process. I noticed in the mirror that I was sweating, but with the vodka I started feeling better. For a brief moment, I regretted not bringing the file along, wanting another look at those photocopies. But I didn't need another look. Without a shred of doubt, that was Marie's hand. Halfway through my second Stoli, I decided she probably didn't even know I was working on the case, whatever her connection might be. But it was possible that she knew. Florian Janicki knew, and there was a good chance they knew each other from Wanda's. I looked at myself staring back from across the bar, damp forehead, baggy eyes, receding hairline, jowls beginning to sag—plenty of other reasons for her to turn me down. Then I wondered where Hollis Lagatee fit into this. The documents had been produced by his office. Is that where the photocopies were made?

Connections. It is for the detective, if he wishes success, to break with the human tendency to dwell upon the solid, to focus upon the thing itself rather than that which connects it to other things. The eye goes to the new coat, the eye goes to the price tag, never acknowledging the little plastic filament which binds them together. I downed my fourth Stoli, mouthed to myself across the bar: *keep your eye upon the hole, Mikey boy, and forget about the fucking donut.* I paid my bill, picked up my car at the LaSalle Hotel parking garage, and drove home to feed Stapler.

I had not eaten all day, yet the colorful, steaming food resting in the rectangles of my Hungry Man dinner, fresh from the microwave, offered no enticement. I left it there, an unspoiled tribute to Mondrian, found a thermometer in the medicine cabinet, popped it under my tongue, staring at my sweating mug while I waited, sure I looked bad enough to scare horses. The silver needle of mercury stopped at 102.3°. I went to bed, resolving to call the doctor first thing in the morning.

I awoke about two a.m. in a rage of nausea, made it to the bathroom, and hugging the cold porcelain I turned myself inside out. I went back to bed, then after what seemed to be an hour I was awakened by a pounding on my front door. I tried to get up and found, to my horror, that I couldn't move. I struggled helplessly, then discovered that I could levitate. I drifted upward, took hold of the ceiling fixture, pulled myself to the doorway, and grasping both sides of the door jamb propelled myself into the living room, where Tadeusz Bartodziec stood purple with rage, screaming in Polish. Marie Galkowska stood behind him, arms folded, jaw set, eyes burning into me. My front door was in splinters. Trying to talk, I was overcome by another wave of nausea. I couldn't help it. I puked on Tadeusz. He began leaping for me, swiping with his short, muscular arms, and caught the collar of my pajamas. Marie was shouting encouragement. I had to puke again. Still paralyzed, I saw his fist coming up in a pulsing of red light and the sound of slamming doors, and then there was only blackness.

Chapter Fourteen

"Mr. Dun-*cavan!* Mr. Dun-*cavan!* Can you *hear me?* Open your *eyes and talk to me!*" Then more quietly, "I think he's awake. Go get Dr. Patel." Now there returned a blissful silence, upon which I began to float back the way I came, and then that shrill voice like a bucket of cold water. "Mr. Dun-*cavan, talk to me!*" A pair of slick oval planes took shape, cruised through my vision, took shape again, eyeglasses, worn by some desperate woman screaming my name. My mind released her, floated back toward the warmth, and then a sudden, jarring shock. Someone was slapping me.

"What the *fuck!*" I said.

A different voice, male, accented. *"Can you hear me? You must answer me. Can you open your eyes?"*

I opened my eyes. Two people were leaning over me, framed against a white, impersonal sky.

"What?" I said.

"Talk to me. Tell me how do you feel." He was dark, with thick lips. Someone was patting my hand.

"What?" I said. It wasn't a sky, it was a ceiling.

"Can you hear me?"

"Will you please stop yelling, for Christ sake," I said. My confused eyes drifted across the room, to a TV mounted up in a corner near the ceiling. They didn't have to tell me it was a hospital room. I was propped up, tubes running in and out of me. I didn't care. I wanted to drift back from whence I came.

"What is your name?" Pause. *"Can you tell me your name?"*

"Mike Duncavan."

"Very *good*, very *good*. Mr. Duncavan, *do you know where you are?*"

"The Jewel?" I just wanted him to shut the fuck up. That did bring a moment of blissful silence. Probably he came from a culture with no sense of irony.

"Mr. Duncavan, who is the president?"

"Charlton Heston," I said. This, again, was followed by a period of heavenly quietude.

Then the female voice said, "I think that's the president of the National Rifle Association, Doctor."

"Mr. Duncavan, can you look at me, please?"

They were not going to let me alone. I opened my eyes once more, looked at the two of them staring back. Then gradually growing more aware, I looked from one to the other. "What am I doing here?" I asked.

"Septicemia," the doctor said. "You had blood poisoning. You were a very sick man when they brought you in." He grinned. "I was afraid we were going to lose you. We've operated on your shoulder, debrided the wound, and put in a drain. How do you feel?"

How *did* I feel? Like existence was an unpleasant chore. Like no one should ever be this sick. "I've had better days."

"You've responded wonderfully to the antibiotics, fortunately for you." Then he said something to the nurse about blood work, and left abruptly.

"Make a fist," the nurse said, tapping the inside of my arm. "Good thing your wife brought you in when she did. Any later, I don't think you would have made it."

"My *wife?*"

She smiled. "You don't remember?" She jabbed my arm with a needle, drew blood into a syringe. "I'm not surprised, your temperature was a hundred-four. You're a

162

lucky man. Here, hold this." She took my finger, pressed it to a piece of gauze at the needle hole, then covered it with a Band-Aid, gathered her things, smiled again, and left me.

I felt too weak to move, sicker than I'd ever felt in my life, but the consensus seemed to be that I was lucky. Lucky Mike, they should call me, just laying here on top of the world. Then with a start, I remembered the investigation, angst bubbling upward in my confusion. I didn't even know what day it was. How long had I been here?

And Beth! How could she have brought me in? She must have taken Stapler. The thought of her was like sunshine after rain. I fought back a creeping fantasy, that this could mean our getting together again. Get real, I thought—the sound of those choirs came only in movies. Still, I recalled the words of Joseph Campbell: *Look to where you stumble, for there you will find your fortune.* Could this be the place?

I slept, dreaming of Beth. I don't know for how long, and when I awoke it was dark. I was feeling markedly better, which enabled me to worry. I had to talk to Artemus. I had to get back to the investigation, to follow up that strange connection, Moses Watson and the Red Eagle Agency and Marie.

What day was it?

I slept again. When I awoke this time, the room was flooded with daylight. A black woman in hospital green, dark-skinned, middle-aged, was adjusting the intravenous apparatus next to me.

"Good morning," she said. "I'm Ms. Barrow. How you feelin' today?"

"There's a bluebird on my shoulder," I said. "Listen, what day is it?"

"It's Friday. You've really been catching up on your sleep, haven't you?"

163

"Friday? Jesus!" I sat up. "What's the date?"

"August eighteenth."

"Wait, that's not possible," I said.

"Maybe not. But it's Friday the eighteenth. Your wife called the desk this morning; she didn't want to wake you. She said if you were awake to tell you she'll be here in a little while."

I sat up, definitely feeling better. "Did she say what time?"

"In a little while," she said.

Ms. Barrow left me, and I lay there ringing with inner hope, anticipating the sight of Beth. Sometimes good things really do happen. Sometimes even I could be lucky.

I must have dozed again. When I awoke, Ms. Barrow was smiling down at me. "Your wife is here," she said, indicating with her hand. I craned my head around to see Beth's face, and my heart froze. There behind her stood Marie Galkowska.

"So, you're still alive," Marie said, when Mrs. Barrow left the room. She was carrying a floral arrangement, which she set down on the bedside table, then fixed me with a perplexed look. "You're not pleased to see me?"

I groped for words. She pulled a chair closer, sat down. Her eyes flickered to the door, then, *sotto voce,* "You were unconscious when we got to the emergency room. They needed consent from a relative to do surgery. I signed. I told them I was your wife."

"But how did you happen to . . . ?"

"You don't remember anything? You called me, completely out of your head. I couldn't get into your apartment, so I talked the cops into breaking down the door—your landlord's not too happy, but he couldn't find the key. Good thing they did. In the emergency room, they didn't think you were going to make it. By the way, your landlord has your dog."

"When did you bring me in?"

"Tuesday night. Actually, early Wednesday morning."

"I guess you saved my life," I said.

"I guess I did. That puts us even. Listen, Mike, I can't stay, I'm on my lunch hour." She kissed me on the forehead. "Oh, one more thing? Please don't try to call me, okay?" And then she was gone.

I lay there awhile, feeling more hollow than the tubes running into me. She'd saved my life, and here I was feeling disappointed that she wasn't Beth. But that wasn't all of it. I still needed to know her connection to the Bartodziec case. It was her hand in those photocopies, there could be no doubt about it. Or could there? From here, tied to all these tubes, I wasn't sure I was looking at the same picture, that it all hadn't been part of my delirium.

Maybe it could be coincidence. Rhinestone nails were common enough. Another woman with rhinestone nails could also have a scar across her wrist. But my gut still told me it was her. And what about the fact that Moses Watson just happened to buy his insurance through Red Eagle? I didn't know what that meant, but I needed to talk to him. I also needed to call Artemus.

When they connected me to Artemus he did not even say hello. "Mike!" he said. "Jesus, where've you been? Discovery closes in five days." A pause. "You missed the Sykes deposition."

I told him I was in the hospital, but I expected to be out soon. When he waxed sympathetic, I asked him to send over the deposition transcript. Then I told him the doctor had just come in, and I had to go, and I called Moses. I didn't tell him where I was.

"Moses, listen, where did you buy the insurance on your building?"

"I think my lawyer got it for me, Mr. McGarry."

I didn't like contradicting him, knowing how his bouts with confusion distressed him, but I said, "I talked to Mr. McGarry. He said he didn't."

He thought for several seconds. "Maybe I got it from the mortgage company. Yeah, now that I think of it, I pay the insurance to the bank when I pay the mortgage; it's all in one payment."

"Moses, listen. You don't have a mortgage any more."

Silence. "Oh, right. No, I send them a check, that's right, to Red Eagle. I don't rightly remember how I got it, though. Maybe somebody come out to the house?"

I thanked him, hung up and called Danny McGarry. When I told him I was in the hospital, I had to talk him out of rushing right over.

"I tried to call you, Mike. I've got good news! Your declaratory judgment idea really got the insurance company off dead center, man. I've worked out an agreement with them. They'll make a substantial payout, as long as we stipulate that they haven't waived any defenses. We've already got a contractor lined up."

That *was* good news. I told him then about Red Eagle and the hand on the photocopies. "Do you have any idea how Moses happened to go to Red Eagle?"

"No. Look, I don't want to tell you your job or anything, but—think about it. It's a big agency. They sell insurance to lots of people."

"You've heard of Red Eagle?"

"Well, yeah, haven't you? They've got billboards all over the place. Hey listen, when you get out of the hospital, why not come stay with me? Maybe you shouldn't be alone, for awhile anyway—God knows I got plenty of room."

"Thanks, Danny, but I think I need to be in the city."

"Well, think about it. You can bring your dog, of course. I been thinking about getting a dog myself. But look here, when you're getting out, call me, okay? I'll come pick you up."

That afternoon a paralegal from Shumway's office dropped off the transcript of Shavonne Sykes' deposition. I sat up in bed and paged through it. Shavonne had two kids, she was on welfare. She used to stay with her mother sometimes. She claimed she had complained to Moses Watson personally, about the broken locks on the front door, said she'd frequently been harassed by panhandlers in the hallways.

There were a few surprises. She said that on July 17th, the night of the shooting, she had been temporarily living with her mother. A little after ten-fifteen, as she was watching the evening news, she heard angry voices in the hallway. She looked out her door, saw two men arguing in the second floor hallway, outside the vacant apartment: a white man and a black man. She had never seen the white man before. She knew the black man only as "Geronimo." He lived in the projects; she did not know what building, or his real name. He was about twenty-five years old, medium build, brown-skinned, with dreadlocks. She did know that Geronimo was a dope dealer. Before the date of the shooting, she had seen him hanging around the vacant apartment, where he'd been dealing dope. The door was usually open, and it looked like people were smoking crack in there. She had not seen Geronimo since the shooting.

When she looked out her door that night, she'd only opened it a crack, and did not step into the hallway. She said she was afraid for her kids. About ten seconds after she shut the door, she heard a shot.

Shavonne said the police came to the door later, and her mother talked to them. Asked why she didn't talk to the police, she said her mother was handling it, and the police never asked to talk to her. She did not leave the apartment at all that night.

Shavonne admitted to having been a heroin addict long ago, but she had gone through drug rehab, and had been off drugs for seven years.

I had no doubt Shavonne was lying, but that didn't mean a jury would see it that way. The fact that she claimed to be temporarily living with her mother would pretty much neutralize Moses Watson's testimony that she didn't live in the building—it was certainly plausible that Moses simply didn't know. And I wasn't sure how Moses, with his occasional memory lapses, would come across as a witness, anyway. I needed to talk to Fannie Walker. She had lived directly across the hall.

Chapter Fifteen

Monday, August 21

On Monday morning I was released from the hospital. I had planned to call a cab, but after getting unsteadily to my feet and wobbling around the room compressed under a mountain of weariness, I called Danny McGarry instead. He was sitting in his car waiting for me at the front entrance when I came out. When he dropped me off, he said, "You're still welcome to stay with me, Mike. Think about it."

I climbed the stairs, fatigue covering me like a membrane, wanting only to slip into my bed, then on the second floor landing I beheld my new front door, for which I did not have a key. I went back down, rang Fred's bell. When he answered, Stapler danced his crazy dance through the door and all over me.

"Fred," I said, a little sheepishly, "I'll pay for the door."

"Not to worry, Mike," he said, handing me the key. Then as an afterthought: "But if it will make you feel better, it was three hundred twenty-nine dollars. That includes installation."

Inside the apartment, I decided against going to bed. I only had the rest of today and tomorrow before discovery was closed in the Bartodziec case. After that, it wouldn't make any difference what I uncovered. We couldn't use it. I knew where Fannie Walker lived, and I needed to talk to her. She was the only one who'd told the police anything about the shooting. She might be able to tell me whether Shavonne Sykes was living in 3 South.

My car had a blaze orange sticker glued to the driver's side window: ABANDONED VEHICLE—POLICE TOW. I scraped off as much as I could with a pocket knife, drove over to Orchard and Willow.

This time Fannie Walker was home. Dark-skinned, late sixties, salt-and-pepper hair pulled back in a bun, she opened her door wearing an apron, a dish towel in her hand, the air filled with the smell of frying food. When I mentioned Moses Watson, she stepped back, asked me to come in, gestured to the couch. I sat. "How is Moses?" she asked.

"He's fine, except this case is eating him up."

"My, that poor man." She frowned. "Seem like it's always the righteous who suffer in this world, don't it?"

I nodded. "What can you tell me about the building? Did he keep it up?"

"It was a nice building. Moses lived on the first floor. He took care of things pretty much," she said.

"At the time of the murder, do you remember if the locks on the front door were broken?"

She looked at the carpet, then at me. "I can't say. Things got broke. Light bulbs burn out, that kind of thing. But Moses always got around to fixing them."

"What about homeless people loitering in the hallways?"

"No, there was nothing like that."

"Strangers asking for money?"

"Inside the building? No, I never saw any."

"Ms. Walker, I know you've told the police everything about that night, but would you mind telling me again what you remember?"

"I don't mind, no, but there's not much to tell. Someone knocked on my door, must've been about ten-fifteen, I was watching the news."

"Knocked on your door?"

"Yes, somebody asking about, did I know when Mr. Watson would be home. I didn't open it. I don't know why anybody'd be asking me about Mr. Watson. I just said I didn't know, and they went away. Then it couldn't of been more than three or four minutes and I heard all this yelling and carrying on. That's when I heard the shots."

This was new, someone coming to her door. "Can you tell me anything about the voice?"

Her eyes drifted. "I don't know. It was a man's voice, that's all I know."

"Black man, white man? Could you tell?"

"Oh, I'm pretty sure it was a white man."

"Did he have an accent of any kind?"

"You mean, like a foreign person? No, I'm sure he didn't. He was polite, said something like, 'Pardon me for bothering you, I'm wondering if you know when Moses Watson will be home.' Like that."

"When you heard the shots, did you look out into the hall?"

She pulled back, frowning and smiling at the same time. "I called the police; that's police business. Ain't none of my business. Could you excuse me a minute? I got something on the stove."

While she was gone I went to the window. This was significant, the man at her door. White man, polite, asking for Watson. Probably not Bartodziec. It meant something.

She came back into the room wiping her hands on her apron. "Can I get you a pop?"

I shook my head. "Ms. Walker, do you know someone named Shavonne Sykes?"

She thought a minute. "Isn't that Mattie Croyance's daughter?" Then without waiting for an answer she said, "I

171

can't say I know her, but she stayed with Mattie sometimes, across the hall from me. Had a couple of kids. Why?"

I saw Moses' testimony, that Sykes never lived there, going down in flames. "Do you remember if she was staying with Mattie the night the man got shot?"

"I certainly don't, it was a long time ago. Yes, I believe she was. They are some strange people."

I didn't say anything, hoping she'd embellish on that. When she didn't, I asked, "Why do you say they're strange?"

She looked at me sideways, not sure she should say it. "Mattie come from Haiti. You ever know people from Haiti? She think she some kind of voodoo priestess or some-thing. She do some strange things."

"Can you tell me what kind of strange things?"

"I'm sorry, I sure can't. I mind my business. Especially where that foolishness is concerned. For awhile, though, they was using the vacant apartment for all sorts of singing and carrying on."

"You mean 2 South? It was vacant?"

"Yeah, it was vacant for a little while, not long. After Calvin Clark died. No more than a month. Long enough for them to bust in there and take it over. One time I even see Mattie going in there carrying a white chicken in a cage."

I was scribbling notes, trying to keep up with her. "Look Ms. Walker, Shavonne said she looked out her door that night and saw two people arguing, a white man and a black man named Geronimo. Do you know Geronimo?"

She shook her head. "Can't say I do, no."

"Do you know if anyone was dealing drugs in the building?"

"No, I don't," she said. Then with a flicker of misgiving in her eye, I thought she was going to change her mind. She said, "I'm pretty sure they were two white men, was arguing."

"Two white men? You're sure?"

"Pretty sure."

"Could you hear what they were saying?"

"No, but the one . . ." She gathered her thoughts. "See, you asked me if the man came to the door was a foreign man. No, he wasn't no foreign man, but I believe the other man was. He was the one mostly doing the hollering, the foreign man."

I thanked her, drove to my office. Physically I was feeling better, keyed up by this new information, but worried that I had so little time. My answering machine had several old messages, two from Artemus, six from his secretary, and a couple from Danny McGarry. They'd been looking for me. That was it. No new cases. It occurred to me, my spirits a little deflated, that this investigation could be my swan song.

Danny called a little later, upbeat, to tell me the remodeling work on Moses Watson's building would start any day now. "I went over there today to let the carpentry guy in."

"Nice to hear some good news." I decided not to tell him what Fannie Walker told me, wanted to mull it over first. He asked me how much time we had before discovery closed.

"Tomorrow's the last day," I said.

"Oh, shit." He made a sound like air escaping his balloon.

I'd assumed he knew—but then the death case wasn't his particular problem. Danny was holding up his end. It was my end that was caving in.

"Looks like we're gonna get this building all fixed up just so we can turn it over to Hollis Lagatee."

"Danny, look," I said. "Even if we went to trial to-morrow, it's still up to the jury." I hung up knowing I hadn't been a very convincing liar. A jury might actually be sympathetic to Moses, but they'd be a lot more sympathetic to the widow and kids.

I called Artemus, reached his voice mail, and pressed zero to talk to the receptionist. She connected me with his secretary. "He's in a meeting," she said.

"Better get him out, Sandie," I said. When he came on, I told him what Fannie Walker told me. "We need to fax new answers to interrogatories, disclose her as a witness," I said.

"Yeah. How helpful is she?"

"She and Norton, the retired CTA driver, both say it was a nice building. But she also contradicts Watson, says the apartment was vacant for a short time. And that Shavonne Sykes actually did live in the building. Buddy, I just don't know."

I called Marty Richter about Shavonne Sykes' arrest record. "It's here waiting for you," he said. He didn't know I'd been in the hospital, and I didn't tell him. I drove over to the Deering station knowing I didn't have time to stop and visit, and I found him in the watch commander's office conferring with two sergeants.

"We're fielding a brutality beef, against one of my best men, actually—sorry I don't have time to talk, Mike." Grateful, I drove back to my office, dog-tired. Dr. Patel had warned me that I needed to get plenty of rest, said I could have a relapse. I thought of calling it a day. Instead, I put on a pot of strong coffee, and when it was ready I sat down at my desk with Shavonne's rap sheet.

Shavonne had not exactly been a model citizen. She had a page and a half of arrests, mostly for possession of a controlled substance, though a couple were for dealing. She'd lied about being free of drugs for five years. There was one conviction less than a year old. She was still on probation for that one.

The convictions might be used to discredit her testimony, but Hollis Lagatee was a master at turning that kind of thing around. He might make her out the victim, paint Artemus as a heartless brute just for bringing it up.

If only I had more time—I'd have liked to get the police reports for each arrest. Were there complaining witnesses? I could talk to them, and talk to the arresting officers, maybe dig up a little more on Shavonne. There was no doubt in my mind: her affidavit was a lie.

I called my friend in police records back, asked if she could get me the case reports from each arrest, if I gave her the RD numbers. While the court file always contained the arrest slip, the full case reports were never included. "Sure," she said. "It'll take a couple of days."

"Is there any way of getting them sooner? It's pretty important."

"No, I'm afraid not." When I turned my chair to the window I saw Sam Miller, the old defense lawyer, heading down Washington toward the Northwestern station to catch the train to Arlington Heights. I looked at my watch—just enough time to get to the court clerk's office before they closed.

At the desk I filled out a request form for the court files on each of Shavonne's arrests, and handed them to the lady behind the counter. She regarded them as she would a handful of spiders. The civil servants in the clerk's office did not look favorably on requests in the last half hour, when they were "getting ready" to leave. I dug into my wallet, palmed a twenty. "These files are all in storage," she said. "Call back in two days to see if they're in."

"Is there any way of speeding this up?" I said, trying to discreetly slip the twenty across the counter.

She appraised me as you would a leper. "Please don't do that," she said, and walked away without looking back. A black guy stood patiently holding the door open for me, and when I went out, the sound of it locking behind me echoed down the corridor.

I headed back to the office, knowing that with discovery closing tomorrow, my race was already run. Not exactly a photo finish. When I reached the front of the building I just kept going, past the Loan Arranger Pawn Shop's inspiring neon to the LaSalle Hotel parking garage. I drove home, considered stopping to eat, decided against it. I was too tired—it was a Hungry Man kind of an evening. At home I fed Stapler, popped a Hungry Man into the microwave, then took my shoes off and fell onto the bed waiting for the microwave bell.

Chapter Sixteen

I awoke with a blade of sunlight slashing across my face and Stapler whining in my ear. I let him out in the yard, then passing the spare bedroom, I felt a sudden urge to work out. From the doorway I looked at the weights and the bags, the speed bag and the heavy one, remembering the doctor's advice to take it easy for awhile, yet sensing that if I didn't work out, I might lose something—lose one more thing. How much was left to lose? And then, a little sorry for myself, it struck me that I had always taken for granted a greater strength: the capacity to rise above self-pity. I got out my bike instead, pedaled over to Lincoln Park, spent an hour working up a lather, and came back feeling pretty good. In the shower, I reflected upon Marie, upon those lovely sculpted nails appearing in the photocopies from the Bartodziec file, and wondering if I had been set up somehow. Was it just a coincidence, meeting her in Wanda's that night?

I shelved that idea, attributing it to my warped, paranoid personality. But before I left for the office, I dialed the Red Eagle Insurance Agency. I was grateful to hear Marie's answering voice, but when she realized it was me, her voice lowered. "I told you not to call me again."

"Hold on, I'm calling on business."

She hesitated, then allowed herself a drop of playfulness. "You mean you want to buy insurance?"

"Yeah, I saw one of your billboards."

"Billboards," she said, and laughed out loud.

It wasn't that funny, but I decided on a long shot. "Really, Marie, I do need to talk to you about a mutual friend, Helen Bartodziec."

She didn't miss a beat. "What about Helen?"

"I need to know how you happened to photocopy documents for her lawsuit."

This time she missed several beats. I waited.

"I have another call, I have to go."

"Marie, wait . . ."

"Look, I'm telling you, don't call me any more. Goodbye, Mike." She hung up.

I thought of calling back, decided to let it cool awhile. I fed Stapler, and was heading out the door for the office when the phone rang. It was Marie. Her tone was icy.

"You are harassing me, Mike, calling me at work. You are going to get me in trouble. So I'm telling you—if you try to call me again, I'm calling the police. Do you understand me?"

"Perfectly." I hung up, wondering if this meant she wouldn't go out with me.

When I got to my office I called the court clerk to see if, by some miracle, the files on Shavonne Sykes had arrived from the warehouse. No such luck. Then Danny McGarry called, in a good mood.

"The carpenters started work on Moses' building this morning, Mike. I went over there myself, to let them in. And you know what? Right in the next block there's two buildings being re-habbed. It's going to be prime property, buddy. The new Gold Coast."

His mood was infectious. I told him what Fannie Walker told me, about the knock at the door, the voices in the hall.

He mulled that over a few seconds. "Hey, cool!" he said.

"It's like, the case is way more defensible than three weeks ago—this could even force a settlement, right? For the policy limits?" He paused. "What do you think our chances are, Mike?"

"I was about to ask you the same question."

"Me? What the hell do I know, I'm a bump and bruiser, a whiplash guy. This is way out of my league."

That surprised me. "What about your quad case, Danny? That was a whole lot bigger than this one."

"Yeah, but I didn't try that myself. What're you, nuts? Joe Power tried it."

I thought a second. So Danny had been the forwarding attorney. He would have taken a third of the fee. A third of a third of, maybe, twelve million?

He asked again. "So what do you think our chances are?"

It was a question I'd been asking myself hourly, especially in the last day or so. "I'd say at best, fifty-fifty. The case is going to the jury. Liability's weak, sure, but there's a big sympathy factor for the widow and kids. And the widow does have Hollis Lagatee. Danny, I don't agree with Shumway about Moses Watson, I'm no longer sure he'll be all that big a hit with the jury. He's too defensive. He'll probably come across as just another slum landlord. Plus, if we use Fannie Walker—and we got to—she directly contradicts Moses about the vacant apartment. Lagatee will make him out to be a liar, to boot."

"But what about her testimony about the two white men? Doesn't that say something?"

"Yeah, it does. With one knocking on her door looking for Moses, it might point away from the shooter being a dope dealer."

Danny was quiet for five seconds. "Well, let's play

179

devil's advocate for a minute, here. All this could still be consistent with Sykes' testimony, right? I mean, let's talk scenarios. This guy Geronimo is dealing dope out of the apartment on the second floor. Okay. Fannie Walker's testimony doesn't negate the fact that Geronimo was there. There could be two white guys there, too. Maybe they don't even know each other. Maybe one's looking for Moses, and the other . . ." His voice trailed off.

"The other is Bartodziec," I said.

"Yeah. I'm lost. So who's looking for Moses, and why?"

"I don't know."

"Maybe it doesn't matter why."

"It matters," I said. "I'd sure as hell like to know what the guy wanted with Moses, a couple of minutes before a guy gets shot in Moses' building."

Danny took a moment to reflect. "You're saying the other white guy shot Bartodziec?"

"I'm not saying anything. I don't know," I said.

"I'm lost," he repeated. "So where the fuck are we?"

"We're pretty much where we started. And who knows how Walker's going to hold up under cross-examination. They've got two shots at her."

"Two? Oh, you mean they'll take her deposition, first, yeah."

"Yeah, and then at trial. Lagatee could have this lady doubting she even lived there."

Danny hung up, no longer upbeat. I had spoiled one more person's day.

I walked over to Artemus' office to give him a final report, wishing I could have given him more, convinced now that he was taking this case personally, that it was his curtain call. And odd as it may seem, he was identifying with Moses Watson, probably needed to win this case more than any in his career. In the green marbled lobby of Artemus' building I pushed the elevator button several times, which naturally made it come faster. At the reception desk the lady dialed, announced my arrival, and asked me to walk back to Shumway's office.

With his back to the broad window, Artemus seemed to be sitting on top of the world. "You've done a great job, Mike. Thanks to you, I'm gonna win this thing, you just watch me." If you didn't know Artemus, his grin might fool you. "Fannie Walker's testimony is what's going to cinch it."

"Artemus—if only we had a little more time."

"Hey, it's not your fault. Hell, it's nobody's fault, we got to work with what we've got, what else can we do? It's not our predecessor firm's fault—they wanted to do the work, the insurance company just couldn't make up its mind to pay for it." Smiling, he came around his desk, laid a hand on my bad shoulder. I tried not to wince. "Listen, old friend, if you want to give me your bill now, I can get a check from accounting for you right away."

It was tempting, but it had an unwelcome air of finality. "Thanks, I'll send you a bill. But maybe I should keep working, what do you think? We've still got sixty days 'til trial."

He shook his head. "What good would it do, Mike? We can't use anything you'd find, anyway."

I shrugged. "It can't hurt."

He shook his head again, went back behind his desk, sat down. "Actually, I've already asked the insurance carrier about that. They won't pay for it." He leaned back, canting his head, gave me a kindly smile. "I'll tell you this, though. I've talked you up at firm meetings, and there'll be plenty of work for you here, if you want it. Maybe you should brush

181

up on your accounting—our commercial guys seem really interested in an investigator who understands a little about accounting principles."

I thanked him and said goodbye, not sure I was the right guy to investigate financial cases, but with no clients beating a path to my door, I resolved to dust off my Basic Accounting textbook.

At my office window, not even the stream of secretaries jiggling past at the end of the workday could lift my spirits. Aware of Beth's picture watching me, I almost turned it to the wall. Then on an impulse, I dialed her number, reached her answering machine. I didn't leave a message. I called Danny McGarry back.

"I was just leaving, glad you caught me. Anything new?"

"I've made my final report to Artemus Shumway. I wanted to know if you felt like meeting me at Monk's Pub for a drink."

"Actually, I'm supposed to meet some people at Fatso's. But hey, why don't you come along? You know what, man? There's this one you should really meet, really hot. You'll like her, she's beautiful, and really bright, too." Danny was talking too fast, his pitch somehow off, and I suspected he'd snorted a line of coke. But that was his business. He was trying to be a friend.

"This hot number—does she, uh, happen to be a lawyer?"

"Well, yeah. But she's in family practice. Why?"

"No reason," I lied. "I'll meet you there."

"Excellent!"

When I started practicing law, woman lawyers were as rare as a Loop parking spot. I didn't mind women lawyers, but I was often mortified, as more and more women came into the profession, by the inability of some lawyers and judges to take them seriously. One incident, during an argument on a motion, was tattooed on my memory: my opponent, a competent, self-assured young woman, had finished her argument. And as I started my rebuttal, the judge interrupted.

"Just a minute, Mr. Duncavan. Young lady, you argue very well, I want you to know that. And as pretty as you are, I don't know how Mr. Duncavan can expect to win."

I felt my face balloon with embarrassment. She was my adversary, she was my colleague. Bonds had been generated, and the judge had rent them, complicating the game. I could not help admiring her cool, though, how she deftly turned aside His Witlessness without giving offense. I was embarrassed for her, for the judge, but mostly for myself, for chuckling mindlessly at the judge's remark. I never had a problem accepting women as lawyers, but I could not seem to accept lawyers as women. Going to bed with a lawyer seemed a lot like going to bed with Danny McGarry.

I decided to stop home, take Stapler for a walk before meeting Danny. But as I crept northward in rush hour traffic, I regretted I'd made the commitment and considered not showing up. Would that create hard feelings? Danny was meeting friends anyway; I probably would not be missed.

As I removed the mail from the box and wearily climbed the stairs, I decided I would not go out again. But as I opened my front door, something happened: the emptiness of my apartment spilled over me like a chill, and suddenly I wanted to be somewhere full of light and human noise. Poor Stapler; he had a very short walk.

Just north of the Loop on Wells Street, Fatso's had lots of brass and polished oak and hanging ferns, and it was packed. Edging my way toward the back, people shouting at each other above the music, I found Danny near the end of the bar, talking to two women perched on stools, their backs to the bar.

"Hey, Mike, I was afraid you weren't coming!" Hand on my shoulder, Danny introduced me. Pam, perky blonde in a violet suit, pink silk scarf, was a second-year associate at an insurance defense firm. She had a pretty, friendly smile; if I'd ever gotten around to having kids, she could have been my daughter. Deirdre was maybe ten years older, pretty but anorexic, pinched face, spindly limbs, hair dark and severely short, in a black suit with a big gold flower pinned to her chest. Deirdre was a divorce lawyer. The circles under her eyes and her underfed look made me wonder whether she was a colleague of Danny's in the White Powder of the Month Club.

"Pam was just talking about depositions," Danny yelled, and moved over, making room. He pressed against Pam's knee.

"Did you ever go to a deposition at Nosbaum's office?" she asked. I could barely hear her above the music. "I was at one today, it really bummed me out. The guy like, read all these stupid questions from this like, stupid list?" She rolled her eyes upward. "And I'm like, God, get ree-yull, okay?"

"Seems like since they limited depositions to three hours, they take longer. Like you're supposed to fill the three hours," Danny said.

"Yeah, like half the questions are even relevant," said Pam. She shook her head. "So-o-o unprofessional."

"Mike, what can I get you?" Danny shouted.

"Double Stoli on the rocks," I said, wishing I'd stayed home and drank with Stapler. Not sure what Danny had told them about me, I had no idea how to talk to these people. Pam seemed to assume I was a lawyer, though even when I was, this kind of conversation turned me blue with boredom. I noticed no one was saying anything. Both women were looking at me. It seemed that Deirdre, whose practice would not involve the same kinds of depositions, and who sat there expressionless except for the sad caste of her dark eyes, was being left out.

"I did a little divorce work when I first started practicing," I said. "Nothing much. Always left custody disputes to the experts. I've heard that divorce practice has changed, though, that now custody disputes are a lot more common."

She smiled with a slight downturn to the corners of her mouth. "It's the world that's changed," she said. "We're climbing out of the dark ages, realizing—finally!—that marriage is a form of slavery." Behind those cold eyes, more animated now, I could see a whole aquifer full of anger, and I sensed she couldn't wait to pump some of it up to the surface.

"Tell him what you were saying before, about the whole first strike thing," Pam said.

Deirdre shrugged. "Lot of lawyers think that all you've got to do is start the ball rolling, file a complaint, then let the settlement take its course."

"And how do you do it?" I asked.

"First thing, you get an emergency order of protection. Get the guy out of the house, make him beg to see his kids. Then he's ready to bargain."

"That's pretty serious stuff, isn't it? Don't you need grounds?"

She grinned. "I can see you don't have that killer instinct. No offense, but if a lawyer doesn't want to go for the jugular, he should stick to real estate closings. Anyway, the

185

orders are always *ex parte*. It's not a problem."

Ex parte, meaning the other side gets no notice of the hearing, so the judge takes everything the petitioner says as if she weren't really lying her ass off.

Pam, sensing she might have steered a course for troubled waters, said, "So, Mike, Danny says you used to be like, a cop, before you were a lawyer?"

I nodded. "But I'm no longer a lawyer, either." If they didn't already know, I thought it was time to make that clear.

"Yeah, I know. Danny said you shot a guy once. How are you with that?"

"Pam!" Deirdre said.

"Sorry, sorry, I can't help it," Pam said, and giggled. "Everybody at the firm calls me the Big Mouth."

I looked from one to the other, both women no doubt finding me more boring than I found them. Suddenly inspired, I reached for my beeper, pretended to examine a number. "Sorry," I said. "I got to find a phone." But I wasn't loud enough.

"What?" Pam said.

"I have to find a phone," I shouted. "I left my cell phone at the office."

Danny motioned with his head. "Back near the john."

At the phone I was out of their line of sight, so I went to the john, instead. I returned shaking my head, looking disappointed. "Sorry, it's just the nature of my business. Duty calls."

"What?" shouted Pam.

"Duty calls!" I said, and gave them a brave smile. As I squeezed my way through the crowd, I saw Danny following me. When we reached the sidewalk, he said, "Mike, I'm sorry about Pam's big mouth. Believe it or not, she's really a talented lawyer."

I waved a hand. "Nonsense. I wish I could stay."

"Wait a minute, Mike. Listen, don't be a stranger, okay?" He hesitated. "I get the feeling . . ." His voice trailed off, but his eyes were level. The nervous staccato his words had taken on, when he'd called me earlier, was gone.

"What?"

"Nothing. If you want to talk, call me, okay? Anytime, day or night. Want to have a drink after work, call me. And hey, don't forget, you're free to camp out at my place any-time."

I thanked him, watched him working his way back through the crowd, and left. Heading home, I picked up Milwaukee Avenue north of the Loop, the taste of that chilled Stoli I'd left untouched on the bar working at my tongue. Wanda's, I thought, was not far. I headed in that direction, thinking about what Deirdre had said. Given the connection between homicide and taking the last thing a man's got, I wondered why more divorce lawyers didn't cash out in a hail of gunfire.

Wanda's was nearly empty, and I took a stool at the rect-angular bar, the two men on the other side sitting in exactly the same place as the first night I'd come here. Wanda came over, took my order, and waiting for her to bring my Stoli, eyes adjusting to the low light, I noticed a couple in a back booth. Then I recognized Marie, facing my way with her eyes cast down. She was with the same man, who was mut-tering in that same tone, all reason. I wanted to get out of there. If she saw me, she'd never believe it was a coinci-dence, and if she was serious about calling the police, nei-ther would the cops. Then her eyes came up and locked on mine and narrowed, fixing me with a stare that blazed with contempt. Her head shook as if she had a chill, and she turned away, exposing a cheek wet with tears. I tossed a ten on the bar and left. With the amount of un-drunk liquor I was leaving on bars throughout Chicago, I could start my own temperance union.

"Stapler, boy, we need a drink," I said, opening the door to my apartment, and by the sweep of his tail and the grin on his face, he thought it was a great idea. I filled a cocktail glass with ice, topped it off with Stolichnaya—with all that ice, it really wasn't that much vodka—slipped into my living room chair, and took the remote in hand. I channel-surfed until it was time for another drink, then channel-surfed some more, until it was time to go to bed.

With the phone jangling me awake, I rolled over to look at the numbers glowing on the clock: two-thirty. I let the answering machine get it. It was Marie, and it sounded like she was crying. I snatched up the phone, trying for a good offense. "If you want to talk harassment," I said, "this is what I call harassment."

"Mike, I'm sorry," she said. "I need to talk to you. Be gentle with me, please." She sounded pretty upset.

"Do you want me to meet you somewhere?"

"No. Let's just talk, is that okay? Look, I think you have the wrong idea about me. I'm not a loose woman. I don't sleep around. The night we met, I thought I was through with the man in my life. You caught me in a moment of . . ." She took two seconds. "Confusion. But I went back to him, so I couldn't see you. I'm not that kind of woman."

So why are you calling me now, I wondered, but I listened, pretty sure I knew the answer: she had broken up with Bozo again.

"Tonight, I'm finished with him for good." She was weeping softly.

I thought of her all alone in her apartment, I all alone in mine, and it was giving me a hard-on—look, I can't help biology. Besides, she was a rejected woman—who was to say that a little comforting wouldn't boost her self-esteem? "Want me to come over?" I said.

"No, you'd better not, I need to think, sort everything out. You probably think I'm a fool, don't you . . ."

"No," I said, then was sorry I interrupted.

". . . you probably think I'll just go back to him." I didn't say anything. "Well I can't blame you, I've gone back to him, and back to him, and back to him. So many times. Wasted my life for him. But no more. This time is different. This is really for good, this time." There were ten seconds of silence. "You asked me about Helen Bartodziec?"

I sat up in bed, switched on the light. "Yeah."

"He—my boss, Roman—he's an ambulance chaser. He steers people to a personal injury lawyer, takes a cut. Isn't that illegal?"

"It's illegal for the lawyer. I'm not sure it's illegal for the chaser." My thoughts raced. Where was she going with this? Could Hollis Lagatee have taken this case from a chaser?

"Well, the sonofabitch is a crook," she said. "He writes people's wills, that's illegal, I know that. And he signs up injured people for his wife's sister's husband, he's the lawyer."

"What's his name?"

"I don't know his name. All I know is, his wife's sister's husband."

"Is it Hollis Lagatee?"

"I don't know. No, I don't think that's it."

"But he sent Helen Bartodziec to this guy?"

She sniffled. "Tadeusz came to see Roman for investment advice, before. Tadeusz wanted to buy apartment

building, and Roman was talking to him about a partnership of some kind. I don't know what happened with that.
All I know is, this lawyer was supposed to help him. Then
after Tadeusz died, Helen brought in his letters and stuff,
and Roman told me to make copies." She paused. "Listen,
Mike, you are a nice guy, I'm so sorry for the way I talked
to you this afternoon."

"You should be," I said.

She chuckled through her tears. "You are a funny man.
Thank you for making me laugh." I didn't say anything.
She chuckled again. "Billboards," she said. "That was
funny."

"It was?"

"A little, bitty agency like us with billboards. I wish.
Maybe they would pay me what I deserve. By the way, how
is your shoulder? Are you taking care of yourself?"

"It still needs your attention."

"If it wasn't for my attention, you wouldn't have gotten
so sick. You should have gone to the hospital that night."

"Tell me more about the Bartodziecs. Were they friends
of yours?"

"I know Helen a little bit from the neighborhood.
Tadeusz, I never really knew him. Just to see him, he came
into the office once or twice. That's all I know, Mike. What
I know is what I told you."

"Can you get me the name of the lawyer? The one he
sends the cases to?"

"Maybe. I think so, yes."

When she said goodbye I switched off the light but
couldn't get back to sleep. I switched it on again, picked up
The Confessions of Saint Augustine, hoping to take my mind
off the Bartodziec case, but it didn't work. I couldn't
imagine Hollis Lagatee paying a chaser for a case. But so

what if he did? It would make great gossip on LaSalle Street, but not one particle of difference in the trial. And anyway, it was over, as far as I was concerned. In the morning, I'd send my bill to Artemus Shumway, and move on to something else. Besides, it wasn't as if Moses had no chance of winning; he had, probably, a fifty-fifty chance. I finally turned out the light.

Chapter Seventeen

Wednesday, August 23

I woke the next morning to rain beating against my bedroom window, and as I drove to the office, the guy on the radio saying something about a polar air mass, sheets of rain whipped my windshield like summer's final curtain. Bumper to bumper, traffic oozed its way along the Kennedy like a slug through a straw, and after parking in the LaSalle garage, I was grateful that it was only a short dash past The Loan Arranger to my building. In my office, I prepared a bill for Artemus, put it in the mail. I didn't have much to do, and at that moment, sitting at my desk watching rain slide down my window and the river of umbrellas drift past below, I was glad of it. But there were two subpoenas I'd served before I'd gone into the hospital, and I wanted to file the returns in court. It was not a big deal; many lawyers didn't bother to file them at all. But I had served them, and I told the lawyer I'd do it.

I put on my raincoat and was going out the door when the phone rang. It was Danny McGarry. "Wish you would have stuck around last night, Mike. It's none of my business, but as one divorced guy to another, you need to get out more. A little female companionship would do you a world of good."

"What makes you think I don't have female companionship?"

"Just a hunch."

"By the way, Danny, I thought you told me Red Eagle

was a big insurance agency, with lots of billboards."

"It is, why? They got a huge billboard right over there on the Kennedy, near Montrose. Red Eagle Insurance Agency, you can't miss it."

"Are you sure?"

"Absolutely positive," he said. "Red Eagle Insurance Agency." He thought for several seconds. "Or maybe it's American Eagle. Why?"

"American Eagle—that's a mutual fund, isn't it?"

I thought the line went dead. Finally, he said, "Well, yeah, maybe. Why?"

"Listen, I meant to ask you last night—how's your declaratory judgment going?"

"Hey, great. We had a case management conference, before Judge Murphy? He really put their feet to the fire, Mike, talking about the insurance company being in bad faith for refusing to pay the claim. He even hinted that the complaint could be amended to ask for punitive damages. I couldn't believe how biased he was—I'm just glad he's biased our way. I really think the company's about to throw in the towel, and it looks like they might pay the whole freight. Thanks for your help with that. Look here, Mike, what say I buy you dinner tonight? Meet you at Nick's Fish Market, five-thirty. Don't say no, you gotta let me do this."

I said I'd be there, then headed out in the rain to the Daley Center. I filed the subpoena returns on the eighth floor, then remembering the files I ordered in Shavonne's criminal cases, and on the chance they'd come in, I took the elevator to the tenth floor. I was in luck; the lady placed eleven files on the counter in front of me.

I went through each one, struck by how few had actually resulted in convictions. There were several "nolles"—short for *nolle prosequi*—the state had simply dropped the charges.

Still more were "Motion state, SOL"—stricken, on leave to reinstate. The prosecution had voluntarily dismissed the charge on the condition they could reinstate it. They did that when they weren't ready and knew they'd lose, though in all my years as both cop and lawyer, I've never known them to reinstate one. In a couple of the cases, Shavonne's lawyer had won motions to suppress—the cops somehow had not dotted an "i" or crossed a "t" and the arrest was thrown out.

There were a few convictions, and not all of them drug-related. Shavonne had served a year in the county jail for Deceptive Practices—too bad the jury in Moses Watson's trial couldn't hear about that one. But even if discovery hadn't closed, it still couldn't come into evidence, because the conviction was more than ten years old. Most of her arrests had been either for dealing drugs or possession of a controlled substance. In one, she must have been busted in a raid, since the arrest slip had the names of a number of others, listed under "Also Arrested." Her most recent arrest, less than a year old, ended in a conviction for selling crack, and she was given probation. Even though we couldn't use it, I asked the lady behind the counter for a certified copy of the conviction. I'd eat the five-dollar fee. Who knew what could happen during trial?

"Are you finished with the rest of these?" she asked.

"I'd like to look through them some more," I said, and while I waited I perused the names of the cops and the prosecutors, looking for anyone I might know. Then something on one arrest slip, the one with several arrestees, caught my eye. Tucked into the middle of the list under Also Arrested was the name: Daniel P. McGarry.

I walked back to my office, the rain having slowed to a few measured drops, and sat with my feet on my desk and the smell of my wet raincoat in my nostrils, mulling over what to do. I caught sight of Beth smiling over at me, and suddenly wished I could talk it out with her. Actually, I could. Beth would listen without interrupting, then tell me what she thought. But calling her would just seem like a pretense, and I didn't really want to put up with Frederick answering the phone.

Danny McGarry had been arrested with Shavonne Sykes, yet he never mentioned to me that he knew her. He'd probably met her around Moses' building, somehow. Moses said he didn't know Shavonne. Or so he said. Could they both be lying? I was tempted to pick up the phone and confront Danny, but I needed to sort it out. There was the possibility that it was a different Danny McGarry. I didn't know Danny's middle name—maybe he wasn't Daniel P. I pulled down Sullivan's Law Directory from the bookshelf, looked him up. He was Daniel P., all right.

The police reports, which are supposed to be a matter of public record, would give the facts surrounding the arrest, but the police department gives them up only grudgingly, and then with so much of the information deleted they're nearly useless. To get the uncensored version, you had to serve the department with a subpoena, wait forever for them to comply, and when they did, they often gave you the censored version anyway. Then you had to go to court for an order requiring them to turn over the uncensored reports. All that takes time, so I feel no guilt in bribing a civilian clerk to get what the police department was legally required to provide in the first place. And I only did that when I was in a hurry. Otherwise, I still had lots of friends in the detective division.

I telephoned my contact in police records, and for the second time that day, luck gave me a rare smile: she had the reports. "If it's okay," I said, "I'll come right over and pick them up."

"What're you, crazy? Of course it's not okay. I'll meet you at the restaurant across the street, eleven forty-five."

It was a long walk to 11th and State, but the rain had about stopped and I had plenty of time, so I took it slow, and my ankle gave me no trouble. From across the street, I spotted her sitting alone in a booth by the window. I sat down across from her, we exchanged pleasantries, then exchanged envelopes, and I walked back to my office. I should have bought her lunch, but I was just about broke. I picked up a Value Meal at Burger King.

Back in the office, burger and fries unwrapped, straw stuck into a Diet Coke, I spread the reports on my desk, found the one covering Danny's arrest. It was disappointing, just the bare-bones. It said the police received information from a reliable informant that drugs were being sold out of a certain basement apartment (a location not far from Watson's building). They got a warrant and raided the place, arrested a number of people, among them Daniel McGarry. Found in the apartment, as well as on the persons of some of the occupants, were quantities of a crystalline substance, quantities of a white powdered substance, and certain drug paraphernalia. Attached was a crime lab report, showing that the substances proved to be rock cocaine and cocaine, respectively. Shavonne was the central character here, Danny just an Also Arrested, charged with possession of a controlled substance. To know more about Danny, I'd have to get his own arrest record, and his own court file. But Danny would only have an arrest record if he'd been convicted, and odds were that he beat this rap, or at worst, got court supervision. In either case, as a lawyer he'd have known enough to get his record expunged. I considered checking to see if he had a rap sheet. It would show if he had any arrests that stuck. But it would take too long, and it would probably just mean running down one more blind alley, anyway.

Alone, I sucked the last of the Diet Coke noisily through the straw, then tossed the remains of lunch into the waste basket. I went back to the case reports, wanting to get an idea of the timing of these arrests. Danny's arrest was not quite a year before Bartodziec's murder—he had known Shavonne a long time, maybe from being around the building. Shavonne's arrests covered nearly two decades, and she'd been arrested three times since the murder, though only one—the most recent—resulted in a conviction. One report showed the date of incident as only two days before the murder. She'd been arrested for selling a controlled substance on July 16th, the day before Bartodziec was murdered. Then it hit me. She'd been charged with a felony, which would have meant a high bond. But according to her deposition, at that time she was on welfare. Did she make bond? If she did, the court file would have a copy of the bond slip, showing the exact date and hour she was released. I hadn't thought to look at that when I reviewed the court files.

I called the clerk's office, asked for the lady who had given me the files.

"She's out to lunch," the guy said.

"Can you tell me, I was in looking at some files this morning. Are they still there?"

"That I don't know."

"Can you just take a look and see?"

"Sir, I just told you, the lady you gotta talk to is out to lunch."

It was raining hard again. I put on my raincoat and

walked over to the courthouse. By the time I reached the tenth floor, the lady had returned from lunch. She still had the files, brought them over to me, laid them in a stack on the counter.

I located the one I needed and, spotting the tell-tale pink corner of a bond slip, my heart sank a little. I snatched it out, searched for the date. Shavonne had made bond, all right: at ten-fifteen a.m. on July 18th—the day *after* Bartodziec was murdered. The night of the shooting, she'd been locked up in the county jail. But there was something else, and it was just as interesting. At the bottom of the bond slip was the signature of the man who bonded her out: Daniel P. McGarry.

And suddenly I remembered something: Moses had told me no one had keys to the building but him and me. But Danny told me he'd let the carpentry contractor into the building to start working, which meant he had a key, too. It looked like Danny and Shavonne Sykes were as close as a pair of tits—there was no longer any mystery about how the voodoo crowd had gotten into the building.

Back at the office, I called Marie. She took me by surprise. "Mike, please don't call me here." Her tone was colder than dry ice. I had a feeling I was dealing with one more turn of the merry-go-round.

"Call you there or call you ever?"

She hesitated. "Wel-l-l . . . ever, I think. Please, you're a nice guy, but . . ."

I waited, giving her a chance to complete that thought. When she didn't, I completed it for her. "But you've gone back to him again?"

"It's not like you think."

"Really? And what do I think?"

"It's different this time. Really, it is."

"No shit? How's that?"

"He's left his wife. He's moved out of the house."

"How do you know?"

"I know. He's got an apartment, I saw it."

So what was the point of my protesting? "Okay. But listen, you said you'd get me the name of the lawyer, the one he sends business to?"

"I can't, not now."

"Look, I promise, Marie, your boss won't get in trouble. And no one will know where the information came from. Just give me the lawyer's name."

She didn't say anything for five seconds, then she whispered into the phone, "Mike, I don't want to tell you now, I'm sorry."

This meant she knew who it was. "It won't affect your boss," I said. "I promise. Tell you what, I'll say a name, you just say nothing if I'm right, okay?"

She didn't answer.

"Danny McGarry," I said.

The silence rang on. "Marie, thanks," I said.

"No, wait. Mike, this doesn't mean I said it was Danny. I didn't say his name, you did. I didn't even agree I would do this."

"Do what?"

"To tell you it was Danny McGarry."

"I know you didn't. You didn't tell me anything. Really, Marie, thanks. And listen, you got my number—if you ever get the urge, call me."

It was time to pay a visit to Shavonne Sykes. I got her address from the answers to interrogatories, then slipped on the shoulder holster and grabbed my sport coat and straw hat from the coat rack.

Shavonne was living on the second floor of a building in

a seedy neighborhood on the south side, and I headed south on the Dan Ryan, got off at 43rd, turned east. Most of the buildings on her block were boarded up, set wide apart among glass-studded lots where other buildings had already fallen. The mail boxes in the vestibule were hanging off the wall, and the inner door was missing. On the second floor, I knocked on the east door. A boy about nine years old opened it.

"May I speak to Ms. Sykes, please?"

Before he could answer, a woman's voice demanded, "Who is it?"

He disappeared toward the back of the apartment. "It's a white po-lice, wants to talk to you."

I waited, looking at a picture on the opposite wall, a guardian angel shepherding two children across a bridge, saw something move at the top of the frame. As I watched, a pair of antennae appeared over the horizon, a cockroach rolled around to the front side, turned and went back. Then Shavonne was framed in the doorway, nipples of her small breasts denting a faded yellow tee shirt. She was dark-skinned, skinny, her hair long and straight and shiny as a crow's wing. There was something else: I had seen her before.

"Yes?" She had a set to her jaw, a challenge, and suddenly I remembered those defiant eyes looking back at me from the Buick in front of Watson's building, the night Errol Flynn had called me.

"Can I come in?"

She thought about that a moment, then stood aside. The living room floor was carpetless, grimy. She didn't ask me to sit down, which was okay with me.

"Ms. Sykes," I said, looking toward the kitchen, "it might be better if we talked alone."

200

"It's okay," she said. "My boy went out. What you want with me?"

"It's about the murder of Tadeusz Bartodziec," I said, and she looked as though I'd just spoken in tongues.

Then light came into her eyes. "Oh, you mean that Polish guy, the court case? Yeah, what about it?"

"You gave an affidavit, and then you gave a deposition, and I need to talk . . ."

She interrupted. "Say, wait a minute, you ain't no police. Let me see your badge."

"I never said I was the police. I'm a private investigator. I just want to talk to you about your testimony."

"I done told y'all everything I know. It's all written down on the paper."

I wondered if she'd already seen a transcript of her deposition. "I'm not sure what you mean," I said.

"They sent it to me, in the mail," she said. "It's all written down. I got no more to tell you, it's all in there." Then, as an afterthought, "You're working on the other side, ain't you? Why should I talk to you, anyhow?"

"Because if you refuse to talk to me, they can bring that out in court. It will look like you're a partial witness."

"Partial witness? Huh! Why shouldn't I be a partial witness? That old man's building was a pigsty. Oughtta put him in jail for keeping a ratty-ass building like that. Look, I'm busy." She turned toward the door.

"Well, I'd like to help you, if you'll let me. See, this is a civil suit. People don't go to jail in civil suits. But people do go to jail for committing perjury in civil suits."

She laughed out loud. "You mean, like they sent President Clinton to jail?"

I shook my head. "You're not the President, ma'am. Besides, the President wasn't already on probation when he committed perjury. Let's see, your probation ends when?"

She looked past me, thought a long time without moving her eyes. Then she shifted them to me. "Look, I don't know what you're talking about." She spoke with conviction, but she didn't move from where she was standing.

"Shavonne, the night Bartodziec was murdered, you weren't at your mother's, you were in the county jail. No sense lying about it—the court records show the exact minute you were released. Tell me something. That name, Geronimo? That's a good one—is there really a Geronimo?"

"I already tole you, I don't know what you're talking 'bout. Now I think you best be out of here." She moved toward the door.

"I bet there really is a Geronimo out there; I can't believe you're that imaginative. But have it your way, Shavonne. If I leave now, I am going directly to the state's attorney's office. And you are going directly to the slammer; that's a lead pipe cinch. If I were you, I'd start finding someone to look after those kids."

She sat down in a chair, slowly rubbed her face in her hands, then stared at the wall for a long time. "You got a business card or something?" she said, still focused on the wall, then looked at me. "Maybe I could think about this, call you later."

I shook my head. "I got to tell you something, Shavonne. Actually, right now I'm really pissed, because I happen to like that old man, and you are lying on him. So, you see, I really *want* to put your sorry ass in jail."

"Just suppose I was to tell you, maybe I really wasn't there that night. What then? If it was a lie—mind, I ain't saying it was one—but if I say I tole a lie, that's whatchacallit. Self-incrimination, right?"

"If you recant before the trial and no one gets hurt, no

one will give a rat's ass. But you know something? I've already got all the proof I need, so I don't really need you to recant."

"Then what the fuck you come up here for?"

"Deal is, you recant, set it straight, *and* you tell me who put you up to this."

She looked at me squarely, gave me a mean little smile. "Goodbye, mister." She moved for the door.

"Fair enough," I said, and started to leave.

She was already closing the door behind me when she said, "Wait a minute." She swung the door open again, went back and sat down, rubbed her face as she had before. Then she looked over at me, arms across her knees. "Can't you give me time to think?"

I shook my head. "Remember: I *want* to see you hit the slammer. So why should I give you more time?"

"Then why do you care who put me up to it?"

"Are you talking, or am I leaving?"

She sat back, stared out the window, shook her head. "I can't go to jail. I got these kids. Who gonna look after my kids?"

"The kids are the only reason you got probation in the first place." I really didn't know that, but it was a good guess. "It's not going to work this time."

She hung her head, then spoke quietly to the floor. "Danny McGarry. Sorry-ass chump—it was his idea. Talkin' 'bout, I can make a lot of money, have a whole better life for my kids. Talkin' 'bout, it's just this one, little thing, nobody's gonna know no different. Sorry-ass, jive-talkin' motherfucker, I shoulda popped a cap in his pale ass when I had the chance."

"Danny's the one who let you use the building for your voodoo meetings, isn't he?"

"Ain't no law against voodoo, mister."

"So you may as well tell me. It was Danny who let you in that building, wasn't it?"

She didn't answer. I let the silence run a bit, then in a softer tone, I asked, "How much did he offer you for your testimony?"

She turned and looked at me with distilled hatred. "Listen, motherfucker, didn't you just make a deal with me? Didn't you just say, 'Deal is, I tell you who put me up to it?' Well I done tole you, motherfucker! I ain't telling you no more!"

I had no doubt Shavonne could easily be pushed to violence. For a second I wondered if there was anything to gain in pushing her over the edge. But I'd gotten what I wanted. And besides, she was right: a deal was a deal. "Okay, but I need you to sign a statement."

"When? It's hard for me to get anybody to watch my kids."

"We can do a short one right now. It might be all we need." I took a three-by-five card from my pocket, wrote on the back:

My name is Shavonne Sikes. I have three children. I was not at home on the night the man was killed in Moses Watson's building. I did not witness anything that happened in the building that night.
Signed _____ Date_____

She read it, then looked at me, exasperated. "You spelled my name wrong. And why you put that in there about my kids?"

"There might be some, you know, sympathy factor," I said.

She took my pen. "Well, I only got two kids," she said.

"No problem, just draw a line through the words and write in what you want."

She lined out "Sikes" and "three," wrote in the corrections, signed her name, and handed it back to me. I said goodbye and got out of there.

I drove back to the Loop, hounded by conflicting emotions. I should have been elated, since I was pretty sure the Bartodziec case was all over. Not one hundred percent sure. With apologies to Yogi Berra, "It ain't over 'til it's over" applies much more to litigation than to baseball. I did have the signed statement, of course. Had I given her time to reflect, she'd surely have reneged, brazened it out somehow, maybe say the date on the bond slip was wrong. Given a little time, she might have even found someone to corroborate that, maybe testify they'd seen her on the street that day. Whatever. Shavonne had been around the block a few times, knew the ropes. Phrases like "self-incrimination," though she may not have grasped the concept exactly, sprang easily to her lips. Still, she didn't see through the old investigator's trick, making deliberate mistakes in a prepared statement. The corrections in her own handwriting made the statement more trustworthy than a whole squad of notary publics.

But then there was Danny McGarry, a guy I'd really begun to like, and the picture of him that was developing was pretty revolting. I looked at my watch: four-ten. I was supposed to meet him for dinner at Nick's Fish Market at five-thirty.

Back at my desk, I called his office, grateful that his secretary said he was on another call. "Would you like to leave a message?"

"Yeah, please give him my apologies. Something's come

up, I can't meet him for dinner. Tell him I'll explain when I see him."

I turned my chair to the window, absently watched the passing stream of foot traffic as I connected all the dots. The picture couldn't be more clear. It had been Danny, after all, who'd arranged for Watson's insurance, through Red Eagle Insurance Agency. I had been too quick to assume that Moses was confused, that his poor old mind had been playing tricks when he'd said it was Danny. Danny, for a short time anyway, had been related by marriage to Marie's boss. The marriage failed, but the in-law connection survived; must have been profitable. Danny steered some insurance business to Red Eagle, Red Eagle steered him some clients, got a split of the fee. I wondered how big a split the insurance agent actually got. And how much was Shavonne in for, for her perjured testimony? How many ways can you cut it? A lot, when all you're doing is farming out cases. Lagatee would get a third of the fee he recovered for Bartodziec's family; Danny would get a third of that. Surely Lagatee had no idea Danny had sold out Moses Watson, his own client; how could he?

And there was something else you could bank on: the two voices Fannie Walker heard in the hallway that night, the two white men—one was Tadeusz Bartodziec, the other was Danny McGarry.

What changes a guy like Danny? If anyone deserved the label "do gooder," it was him. What was the music he'd heard from across the wall, what made him cross over, abandon everything his soul was made of?

As I pondered what to do next, the phone rang, and in that instant I had a flash of inspiration, and I let the answering machine get it. "Hey, Buddy," Danny said, "I'm disappointed you can't make it. But I'll be at Fatso's later, if you want to stop by. Listen, come, will ya? You really need to get out and have some fun, for Christ sake. Hope to see you. Bye."

The idea lit up my brain like a strobe light, almost too bold to work. There wasn't much time. I'd confront Danny first thing in the morning. Now I took the Bartodziec file from the cabinet, removed the envelope with the crime lab photos, and sat staring at the magnified firing pin impression in the spent cartridge, its elliptical shape like a small trench—one more connection in the weave of this case, one I should have spotted before.

I called a copy service, asked if it was possible to get laser copies of photographs on a rush basis.

"Sure, how soon do you need them?"

"I'd like to bring them over and wait for them, if you can do it."

"We don't usually do that—hang on a minute, please." He put me on hold, came back about twenty seconds later. "How many are there?"

"Just two. I need two of each."

"If you can bring them right over, no problem. But we close at five."

Then I retrieved two envelopes, a regular letter-sized one, and an eight-by-ten manila, from my desk drawer. I put the small one in the manila envelope, along with the photos.

It was a four-block walk to the copy service, and as I sat waiting for the copies, it suddenly hit me that Shavonne might try to warn Danny—why hadn't I thought of that? I couldn't wait until tomorrow to confront him. I asked a woman sitting at her desk if I could use her phone, then went around the counter, dialed Danny's number.

"Mike!" he said when he picked up. "I didn't cancel the

reservations yet. Can you make it?"

"I can't, Dan. But I need to talk to you about some-thing."

"Hey, why don't we talk over dinner?"

"I can't. Can I just drop by now?"

"*Mi casa es su casa,* buddy. What's going on?" He was in a good mood, though he seemed a little manic.

"Tell you when I get there."

"Hooooo, sounds mysterious," he said. I was pretty sure Shavonne hadn't reached him. Since she'd ratted him out, she might not even try, but I couldn't take that chance.

By the time I got the copies and paid for them, it was after five. They were in the copy service's envelope, with the original, and I took one copy, folded it in thirds, put it in the small envelope. I slid the other one flat into the ma-nila envelope.

I stopped back at my office just long enough to tuck my portable Dictaphone into the breast pocket of my sport coat, then set off to meet with Danny. I found the glass outer door to his office locked, the reception area in the gloom of semi-darkness. I reached into my breast pocket, slipped the Dictaphone button to "record," and rapped on the glass. In half a minute Danny appeared, with a big, glassy-eyed smile. He must have just done a line of coke.

"Hey-hey," he shouted, unlocking the door. "Come on back and tell me what's so mysterious." His voice had that off-key quality I'd heard a few days before. I followed him, seemingly smaller somehow, to his office. He plopped down behind his desk. "Sit down, Mike." He gestured toward a chair. "So what's going on?"

"Just wanted to show you something, from an investiga-tion I'm working on. Thought you might get a kick out of it, being the frustrated cop that you are."

He laughed. "Okay, guilty," he said. "So whatcha got?"

I sat in one of the two chairs, laid both envelopes on his desk. He sat forward, curious.

"This is a blowup of a firing pin impression on a spent cartridge," I said, pulling the copy from the manila envelope. "Notice anything?"

He studied it, then slowly shook his head. "No. Other than it's from a .45 automatic. What am I supposed to see?"

"The impression's elliptical. Only one make of gun in the world makes an elliptical impression like that. Know what it is?"

He shrugged. "No idea."

"Well, guess."

He smiled, gave me a quizzical look. "No clue," he said.

"Oh, come on, Dan, take a guess. What kind of pistol do you shoot?"

"A Glock?"

"Bingo, Dan," I said, watching his eyes. He was still smiling, but he shifted, a little uncomfortable.

"Now let me show you something else," I said, pulling the other copy from the smaller envelope, unfolding it, laying it next to the first one. "Here's a picture of another casing. Notice anything?"

He studied them with his brow furrowed, eyes darting from one to the other. "They look like they're the same," he said.

"Bingo again, Dan," I said.

"Hey, cool." He sat back smiling, but his eyes were a little puzzled.

"This one," I said, hammering a finger hard on the one on the left, "came from the gun that killed Bartodziec."

His smile was gone now. "Mike," he said, "you seem to have an attitude, here. What the fuck are you doing?"

"I talked to Shavonne Sykes today, Dan," I said, and then, watching his eyes, I let the silence run on.

He shifted, cleared his throat. "Yeah, so?" I didn't say anything. Beads of sweat started popping out on his forehead. Finally he said, "Look, Mike, you're beginning to piss me off, here. What the fuck is going on?"

"I should have guessed how Shavonne, Lagatee's star witness, and all the voodoo folks were getting into Watson's basement. You're the only other person who had a key. It's pretty obvious why you needed to stay in her favor."

His eyes darted like a trapped animal, at once fierce and frightened. "Look, you got something to say to me, Mike, goddammit, say it."

"Shavonne told me about your scheme, Danny, about how you bought her testimony. I know all about it, about you being the referring lawyer on the Bartodziec case. See, the night Bartodziec was killed, Shavonne was locked up in the county jail—her bond slip says it all. She's on probation, and she doesn't want to go to the slammer, so she gave me a written statement." I didn't say he wasn't mentioned in the statement, but I didn't say he was, either. "I don't get it, Danny. How could you sell out your own client? I mean, Jesus. Anyone in the world but you."

He pushed back in his chair like I'd slapped him, and his eyes flared with anger, and he stared at his desktop with that angry expression. Then his chest bucked a little, as though he were stifling either a laugh or a sob. When he looked up at me, his stare was full of anguish. Then he spoke, his voice low, his words measured. "Did you hear what you just said? Do you *know* what you said? 'Anybody but you?' Cuz that's it, buddy, the fucking story of my life." He was fighting back tears now. "Danny the good kid. You know when I was growing up, other kids got in trouble, nothing happened to them. I would jaywalk, the whole neighborhood was shocked. 'Not Danny McGarry. We expect more of Danny.' Danny, the perpetual altar boy, the kid who got up at five-thirty every morning and froze his nuts off walking to church in the dark, to serve six-thirty Mass. Because I couldn't bear the censure if I didn't, from my parents, from the nuns. When I went to a dance, I always danced with the ugliest girl there. You know why? Because I couldn't stand the pain of watching her humiliation, standing alone and ignored and not knowing where to look.

"How much time did you give to pro bono work when you were practicing, Mike?" I didn't think he wanted an answer, so I didn't give one. "How much time?" I started to answer, but he interrupted. "Well, I'm tired of carrying everyone else's weight. It's my turn, now, so fuck the world."

His eyes searched his desk top. He started drumming his fingers. Then his hand went to his left top drawer. "Please, Mike, I need this," he said. He pulled it open, withdrew a plastic bag of white powder, carefully shook some onto the smooth surface of his desk. I let it go—what else could I do? He rummaged in the drawer, found a single-edged razor blade and a plastic straw, husbanded the coke into a line with the razor blade, then snorted it through the straw. He sat back, eyes squeezed shut, pinching the bridge of his nose. When he opened his eyes they were red and watery, and he blinked several times, then opened his mouth as though he were about to sneeze. After a few seconds, he seemed to gather himself, solidify.

"Just tell me, Mike. What the fuck is this about, these photographs?" His voice, louder now, was edged with anger.

"This is what it's about," I said, pounding my finger on the second photo. "This one came from your gun."

He squinted at me. His mouth opened and closed. "Wait a minute, you're full of shit. How could you . . . ?"

"Dan, I'm not playing games, here. Remember that bag of brass you gave me? The one on the right, it came out of that bag. Look again. It's identical to the one the police found in the hallway."

His eyes dropped to the photos, returned to me, went back to the photos again.

I said quietly, "Why don't you tell me what happened that night?"

He sat back heavily, closed his eyes, and for a moment was perfectly still. Then he slowly rotated his chair away to face the window. When he didn't say anything, I said, "I know you went with Bartodziec to Moses' building that night. I know about the partnership deal."

"What partnership deal?" he asked, his voice low, still looking out the window.

"Look, I'm holding all the cards, so don't fuck with me. Bartodziec wanted to invest in real estate, and you were working with him on a partnership deal, I know that."

He rotated his chair slowly back to face me. "Okay. It was an accident, Mike. It was self defense."

"No shit? An accident *and* self defense?"

"Yeah, it was both. I thought a partnership was win-win for everybody, you know? Moses was strapped for cash, the building was going down, he was constantly in housing court—this was before the fire, remember? He couldn't even pay my legal bills. I got tired of carrying him, figured if Bartodziec threw in the cash, I did the legal work, and Moses deeded in the title, we'd have a partnership. Even-Steven. I took Bartodziec there that night to introduce him to Moses, explain the deal to them, but Moses wasn't home."

212

"Wait a minute. You never told Moses about this?"

"I was a little high that night, okay? I wasn't thinking straight. I'm explaining the deal to Bartodziec while I'm showing him the building, we're standing in the hallway, and all of a sudden he gets all huffy, wants to know why I should get a third just for doing a little legal work. A little legal work! Shit! There had been a time I really felt sorry for Moses Watson, you know? I never pushed him when he didn't pay my bills. But Moses and his building turned into a fucking albatross around my neck. If it wasn't for him and his fucking building . . ." His eyes drifted a moment. "It was Shavonne got me started on cocaine again, you know that? I got the habit at Notre Dame, but I went through the program, I kicked it. Then I meet up with Shavonne—in fucking Moses Watson's fucking building, where else?"

I tried for a sympathetic tone. "Danny, tell me what happened that night."

He let out a long rush of air, seemed to collapse into himself like a water toy deflating. "Like I said, Bartodziec gets all huffy, tells me I'm trying to cheat him. We're in the second floor hallway, and he starts to walk away. I stand in front of him, telling him wait a minute, hear me out, and he shoves me aside, heads for the stairs. He's yelling in Polish, and I grab his arm, trying to reason with him. I mean, he came in my car, he had no way to get home. So he turns around and punches me in the face. Now I'm pissed, so I take a swing at him, and suddenly he's punching the shit out of me, going nuts, screaming his head off. I pulled the gun, just to scare him. I mean, it was bad, Mike, I was taking a serious beating, and he wouldn't quit. The gun went off. It was an accident."

I didn't believe him, the part about it being an accident. The Glock was a double-action pistol, requiring some force to pull the trigger; it wouldn't just "go off." But I decided to let it go. He'd stopped talking, his face seeming to harden, but his eyes drifted again. Hands shaking, he snatched the bag of powder, shook more onto the desk, some of it falling onto the carpet. He raked it into a line, snorted it up through the straw.

"Jesus," I said, "you better lay off that stuff."

He sat back, eyes closed, his head sinking into his shoulders. His eyes blinked open. He looked at me. His eyes narrowed.

"What're you going to do, Mike?" Before I could answer he was on his feet, leaning on his hands over the desk. "I want to know what the hell you're going to do."

I kept my voice calm. "I think you better chill out . . ."

"So what the fuck you gonna do?" His eyes were wild now, unfocused. "Cuz I can't go to jail, that's that. What the fuck you gonna do, Mike?" he yelled.

I stood, keeping my voice calm. "Danny, sit down and think about this. Try to settle down, will you? That shit is frying your brain."

"You sit down!"

"Now, wait a minute . . ." I held up a hand, starting to get mad.

"I *told* you to sit down," he yelled, then yanked open the right hand drawer, and there it was, the Glock .45, suddenly in his hand, and he pointed it, the dark eye of that muzzle as big as a quarter and looking straight at me.

I sat down, patting the air with both palms. "Danny, believe me, you're out of control. Just put the gun down." My own revolver was in the shoulder holster under my arm, but did I want to shoot Danny? No. But then, if it was the only way to save my own pathetic ass, hell yes. Close as my revolver was, though, I wasn't about to reach for it. It might as well have been back home in the closet.

"You motherfucker, *answer me!*" With his left hand he jerked the slide back, chambered a round, pointed it with two hands at the middle of my chest. I felt my butt pucker. And Danny's hands were trembling.

"Okay, let's just talk," I said, trying to stay calm. "You tell me, what do you want to do?"

"Don't patronize me, motherfucker!" He thrust the pistol at me, eyes wide, pupils dilated. We stared at each other across the desk. If only I could get closer—but the desk stood between us like the great wall of China. Then his chin started to tremble, and he closed his eyes and he sobbed and melted down into his chair, the hand holding the gun falling to his side. I let him sit like that a minute, his shoulders now and then shuddering, tears streaming down his face.

Finally I said, "Danny, would you please give me the gun?" I got to my feet real slow, but he took no notice. He dropped his chin to his chest, shook his head slowly. I thought at first he was telling me he wouldn't hand it over, then I realized it was utter bewilderment. "I'm so sorry," he said quietly. "Really, so sorry. Here, Mike." Without looking up, he thrust the gun toward me.

And then it went off. In a deafening explosion, the bullet crashed into my chest like a blow from a baseball bat, and I reeled backward, my head crashing into something. I must have lost consciousness for a moment. I was on my back, staring at the ceiling, every breath bringing lightning strokes of pain across my chest. Danny was kneeling next to me, sobbing. "No! No! No! Oh, God, oh, God! Oh, please God, no, no! Mike, talk to me. Please, please! Talk to me!"

But I couldn't talk. Breathing, even shallow and rapid, hurt like hell. Then Danny was dialing the phone, and seconds later yelled, "There's a man been shot, hurry." He gave his address and suite number, then he knelt down next to me again. "I gotta get out of here, Mike. I'm so sorry. I'm really, really sorry." And he was gone.

I lay there awhile staring at the ceiling. Then with one massive heave of the will, I rolled to my left side. The pain was brutal, and I rested a minute, moving a hand tentatively inside my sport coat. My fingers came back sticky with blood, but there was something else. Bone fragments? No, pieces of broken plastic. The bullet had smashed my tape recorder. I got to my knees, then grabbing the desk, gained my feet, the effort causing deeper breaths, each one a ball bat across the chest. I sunk into the chair.

"Hello," someone yelled. I didn't even try to yell back. A young policeman looked in the door, and then the paramedics were putting me on a stretcher.

Probing gently around the entrance wound with gloved fingers, the emergency room doctor suddenly pressed hard and squeezed.

"Fuck!" I yelled, and tried to sit up. The nurse put a hand to my bare shoulder, urged me back down on the gurney.

The doctor withdrew something. "Relax," he said, holding up a bloody shard of black plastic like a trophy. He dropped it in a tray, ran his hand along my chest under my arm, palpated a painful bulge near my armpit. "I think that tape recorder in your pocket took most of the energy from the bullet. I can feel it here, under the skin. I think you've got some cracked ribs, though, that's why it hurts so much when you breathe. We're going to give you something for pain, and get some X-rays, but I think you're okay."

The nurse gave me a shot, and they wheeled me to Radiology. When they brought me back, a detective in a rumpled sports coat and a Bugs Bunny tie was waiting for me in the draped cubicle. I sat up, started to get down off the gurney. Whatever they gave me had taken away most of the pain, and I felt awkward lying there while this guy, a younger version of myself, questioned me. In another lifetime, I had stood in this same cubicle in this same hospital, asking the same questions. But I never would have worn a tie like that.

"Maybe you should just lie down," he said.

"It's okay," I said, but a nurse, who must have heard us, swept back the curtain.

"You have to lie down," she said. She stood there until I complied, but as soon as she left, I sat up with my legs hanging over the edge of the gurney, as he jotted down what I told him on a clipboard. I don't think he believed me at first, about faking Danny out with the photocopies of the spent shell, but finally he said, "You got some balls, you know?" And all I could think of was, yeah, but at this rate, for how long?

As he left, the doctor was scanning X-rays he'd stuck up on a shadow box. "Look here, Mr. Duncavan," he said, pointing to a bright white clump at the edge of the rib cage. "It doesn't look like the bullet penetrated the chest wall; it was deflected by your tape recorder. It's got to come out, but we can do it tomorrow, under a local. It's no big deal. You've got two fractured ribs here," he traced a finger over some ribs, "but they're non-displaced, so that's no big deal, either. They just take time to heal. Breathing is going to hurt for awhile, though. I'll give you something to take for pain." He gave me a big smile. "You're going to be fine. We need to keep you for a day or two, just in case. You know," he said, "you are a very lucky man."

217

They wheeled me down this corridor and that, light fixtures streaming overhead like stripes on a highway. Lucky Mike! It's no big deal! For the second time in a week, I was flat on my back in a hospital, and the world seemed to envy my great fortune. How unfair, that such an abundance should bless a single human being. They pushed me into an elevator, brought me up to a room, a nurse came in, gave me another shot, then shut off the lights. I closed my eyes, and slept the sleep of the just.

In the morning, a nurse's aide brought me some pills that made me feel almost happy to have been shot. I picked up the bedside phone and called Fred, my landlord, told him I wouldn't be home for a day or two, asked him if he'd look after Stapler. I didn't tell him where I was. At eight-thirty I called Artemus.

"Mike! Jesus, are you okay?" he said, which confused me, since he couldn't know I was in the hospital. Then he said, "You're at Mercy, right? Can you have visitors?"

"I'm okay, Artemus. I should get out by tomorrow." I was puzzled that he knew I was there, and I didn't know where to begin telling him about Danny, about how he'd shot Bartodziec. "Listen, I've got a lot to explain. We need to file a motion to dismiss."

"Explain? Man, haven't you seen the news? It's all over radio and television. You're headlines in all the papers, buddy. By the way, they keep saying you're in fair condition—how the hell are you, really?"

"Really, I feel like tap dancing. I think it's these pills they keep giving me. But listen, Artemus, you need to file a motion . . ."

"Mike, forget about the case, will you? The case is over. Hollis called me this morning, all apologetic. He's presenting an emergency motion for voluntary dismissal." He laughed. "He asked my permission to do it by agreement, so I wouldn't have to go."

"Did you give it? You can probably get your costs back," I said, only half-joking.

"Nah, who wants to fool around with that stuff? Besides, who's gonna pay, the widow? Lagatee had his hat in his hand, though. Pompous bastard, I loved it."

"Well, now the widow's got a great case," I said. "Against Danny McGarry."

"Naw, the statute of limitations has run."

"No it hasn't, Artemus. Think about it. So long as the cause of action's been fraudulently concealed, the statute doesn't run. You couldn't find a better case for tolling the statute."

"Hey, you're right—but I don't think McGarry's malpractice insurance will cover this."

"I don't know about malpractice, but he's got liability coverage. Remember, he's claiming it was an accident. As long as he sticks to that story, the company's got to cover him. And don't forget, he's got a house in Barrington that's paid for. Helen Bartodziec and the kids can take that, for starters."

When I said goodbye and replaced the receiver, I found the TV remote control on the bedside table. Apparently my landlord hadn't heard, but then he rarely watched TV, and he didn't get the papers. I surfed the channels until I found CLTV news. They were covering the story, with footage of the outside of McGarry's building, then a shot of his name on his office door. Now the reporter was saying, "McGarry is a suspect in the shooting, in his office last evening, of former attorney Michael Duncavan. According to police, Duncavan is now a private investigator. Duncavan is listed in fair condition at Mercy Hospital. Back to you, Jeff."

The anchor came on. "We've just received word that attorney Daniel McGarry has surrendered himself to detectives at Area One police headquarters, in the company of his lawyer." They went to a commercial, and I clicked it off. Suddenly, even under the influence of those pills, I was feeling a little down. It was all great, but it was over. So where did I go from here?

I must have dozed. When I awoke I noticed, from the corner of my eye, someone watching from the door.

"I didn't want to disturb you," Beth said, and at the sight of her, framed in the doorway holding a bunch of roses, a squirt of joy shot through my heart. "So, anything new in your life?" she asked.

"I'm thinking of buying a hospital room," I said. "A kind of condo here, it might be cheaper."

She came over, kissed me lightly on the forehead, then unwrapped the flowers, arranged them in a vase on the table. "They're from my garden," she said. "Actually, they were Frederick's, but he's gone, so I don't think he'll mind."

"Frederick's gone?" I said.

She took my hand, smiled that radiant smile, then kissed me on the mouth, her lips lingering a moment. She straightened, nodding twice. "To Atlanta, with Howard. We finally found a minister who'd do a gay marriage. Unitarian, a very nice man, we had the ceremony in my garden. It was so beautiful, Mike, you should have seen the two of them, under a white canopy, garlands of roses everywhere. Howard's an artist, too, you know. Too bad you never got to know them." She stroked my hair, and then she kissed me on the lips again, slower this time.

About the Author

A Chicago trial lawyer, Thomas J. Keevers is a former homicide detective with the Chicago Police Department. His short stories have appeared in literary magazines and anthologies and been featured on National Public Radio's "Stories on Stage."